THE ART OF

Wind Playing

THE ART OF
Wind Playing

by ARTHUR WEISBERG

Schirmer Books
A DIVISION OF MACMILLAN PUBLISHING CO., INC.
New York

Collier Macmillan Publishers
London

43520

Macmillan Publishing Co., Inc.
866 Third Avenue, New York, N.Y. 10022
Collier-Macmillan Canada Ltd.

First printing 1975

Printed in the United States of America

Library of Congress Catalog Card Number: 74-33818

CONTENTS

PREFACE

This book has been written to further the cause of wind playing. In spite of a few great players, wind playing is in a rather primitive state. The development of the wind family has been quite different from that of the other important families of instruments—the strings and the keyboard. The greatest development of the string family started with the Cremona period in about 1600, while the winds did not attain a high degree of perfection until the first part of this century. Almost all the early Baroque and Classical composers played the violin, and many were the leading virtuosos of their time. This was also true for the harpsichord and later the piano. It is no coincidence, therefore, that most of the great music of the Western world has been written for strings or keyboard. For until recently it was the intrinsic sound of the strings and keyboard that came to represent the ideal of musical sound. All this is a direct result of the early perfection of these instruments and the consequent high level of technical excellence achieved by the players in their efforts to exploit this perfection.

The "built-in" acoustics of the strings and piano automatically lead to what we have come to accept as a "naturally musical sound," because of the *natural* resonance which occurs at the end of a string note and which is completely missing from the winds. The term "resonance" is used to describe the behavior of the sound as the note ends, rather than to describe the tone quality during the time that the note is being sustained. The string instrument is resonant in this way because both the individual string and the body of the instrument continue to vibrate for a short time after the bow has been lifted from the string. This kind of resonance is completely missing from the winds because they are purposely made thick and stiff, and add virtually no vibrations of their own to the sound. The way in which the wind instruments are made and the materials of which they are made have an effect on tone quality, but not on the resonance. If we accept, as does the author, that resonance is an important part of the musical experience, then wind players must learn how to incorporate it into their playing.

A consistent pedagogy does not exist for winds as it does for the strings and the piano. One reason is that the most important and basic aspects of wind playing take place completely hidden from view, inside the lungs and closed mouth of the player. This is in marked contrast to the situation on the strings and the piano. Also, many of the newer techniques are not yet in widespread use; for example, vibrato and double-tonguing are completely unknown to many players. In addition, the style of playing differs greatly from country to country, much more so than for the strings; this is true not only for playing, but also for the actual construction of the instruments. Furthermore, wind players do not go very deeply into certain of the techniques that are considered essential on the strings; string players must master many different kinds of bowing, but the wind player is content with two or three different kinds of tonguing, the use of the tongue and air being the equivalent of the bow. It is no wonder that string players feel themselves to be musically superior to the wind player. The great wind players are the ones who have, consciously or unconsciously, learned to imitate the sounds of the strings. As we shall see, all this is a matter of technique. Of course technique alone does not make a great musician. Ultimately it is up to the individual and what he has to express that will determine how great a musician he will become. This expression depends on a thorough knowledge of the techniques of musical language. It is these techniques and their application that are the subject of this book.

ARTHUR WEISBERG

PART *I*

TECHNIQUES

CHAPTER 1

DYNAMICS AND INTONATION

All aspects of wind playing fall into four main categories: These are: (1) finger technique, (2) the use of the tongue, (3) the use of the air, and (4) the embouchure. It is the third and fourth of these that are responsible for dynamics and intonation. Before beginning the discussion, a few things will be taken for granted. These are that the player is using the correct fingering and that his instrument is more or less in tune. It is also necessary to assume that he has a fairly good reed, since the reed can have a drastic effect on the intonation. As far as the embouchure is concerned, there are very many different types in use. They vary considerably from player to player and from country to country, and therefore it is not possible to go into specific ones. The main point for us to realize now is that once the particular embouchure has been decided upon, it is its use and the use of the air that are the ingredients of dynamics and intonation.

If we look back to the Renaissance, we find that most wind instruments had fixed mouthpieces. The player could not change the way in which the mouthpiece performed

3

its function. For example, there were reed instruments in which the reed was placed inside a tube so that the player's lips could not touch it. There were also reed instruments in which the player put the entire reed in his mouth and did not touch it with his lips at all. The recorder had a fixed mouthpiece. The significant fact for us is that none of these instruments could play more than an extremely narrow range of dynamics. Some could play loudly and others softly, but they could not mix these dynamics because they could not alter the effective size of the reed. Depending on the type of reed (this also includes the recorder), only a particular amount of air would cause it to start to vibrate, and any deviation from this would cause the note to be out of tune, or to stop completely (on the recorder, the note could jump an octave). These reeds were also quite primitive in construction, mainly because they were not called upon to play in a more subtle way. From these facts, we can draw our first major conclusion, which is that the embouchure and the air are completely interdependent. It is not possible, for example, to change from one dynamic to another by altering only one of the two; both must change.

Dynamics

A reed imparts its vibrations to the air through the instrument. The greater the amplitude of these vibrations, the louder the sound. In terms of the reed this means that, in order to be louder, the vibrations of the reed must cover a greater distance. Therefore, the natural opening of the reed becomes the limiting factor in attaining the loudest dynamics. All other things being equal, the reed with the greatest opening will produce the loudest sound. On the clarinet, this means that the mouthpiece that allows the greatest distance between it and the reed will produce the loudest sound. Any closing down of the reed by the embouchure will limit the loud dynamics, so that if one wants to play loudly one should close the reed as little as possible. This can be demonstrated on the bassoon by playing a note with the reed taken completely into the mouth so that the lips do not touch the vibrating part of the reed at all. The player will be surprised to find out how much air is required to make the reed vibrate and how loud the note is. Of course it is not possible to play this way, but the demonstration can show how to play a really loud note, and we are actually more interested in the principle, which is to allow the reed to open more and more the louder one wants to play. One can actually approach the "no embouchure" way of playing by keeping the embouchure very loose. Many students, when they try this, find themselves playing louder than they thought possible.

For the softest playing, the reverse situation is true; that is, the reed must be closed as much as possible. Figure 1 shows a bassoon reed at three widely separated dynamics.

fff   *mp*   *ppp*

Figure 1.

Our palette of dynamics therefore depends on the opening of the reed. In order to have the greatest range of dynamics, we must be able to use the complete range of openings available on the reed. Notice that at *ppp* only the tiniest sliver of an opening remains in the reed.

Thus far, we have been talking about dynamics only

5

in terms of the opening of the reed. The other factor is the air. The reed is a mechanical device designed to vibrate. It is the action of the air going through the blades of the double reed, as the bassoon and the oboe, or through the single reed and the mouthpiece, as in the clarinet, that causes it to vibrate. Given a particular opening, the reed will not start to vibrate until a critical quantity of air is going through it. This quantity of air is solely dependent on the size of the opening. Of course we must realize that for a harder, stiffer reed, the critical quantity would have to be greater. If we refer to Figure 1, we can see that *fff* requires a great deal of air, *mp* less, and *ppp* hardly any at all.

Many players are limited in how softly they can play because they do not realize that the reed can be closed down to practically no opening, or that in such an extreme closing of the reed it is also necessary to cut the air stream down to almost nothing. Figure 2 shows the relationship between air and embouchure.

Figure 2 presupposes an ideal situation—that is, that the reed is perfect, a situation reed players will assure you does not exist. Therefore, in reality it is not possible to achieve such a complete range of dynamics, at least not on every note of the instrument. For example, on the oboe and bassoon, the lowest few notes can rarely be played below a *pp,* no matter how much the opening is closed, or how little air is used. This is because each reed has its limitations as to how much air is necessary to make it vibrate. We must realize that each reed is a tremendous compromise. If we look at the strings, we see that they divide the range among four strings, each of a different thickness. This is not only because the fingering would be extremely difficult on one string, but also because the tone quality would suffer greatly if a thick string were played

6

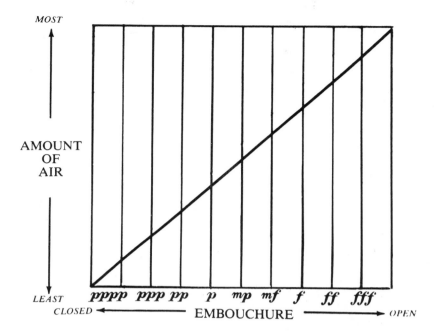

Figure 2.

on high notes or a thin string on low ones. It is the same with the reeds. What is really needed is a small reed for the high notes and a large one for the low notes. The player simulates this by closing the opening for the high notes, which also has the effect of damping some of the lower vibrations. This allows less of the reed to vibrate, and effectively makes it into a smaller reed. On the flute, the player uses his lips to change the size of the mouthpiece opening. But in any case, each reed, because of the way it is constructed, favors a different register of the instrument. Within that range it can approach the outer limits of dynamics, while outside that range it is more or less limited. Players learn all kinds of tricks to extend this dy-

7

namic range but are ultimately limited by the particular reed.

Intonation and Pitch

So far we have only been speaking of dynamics, which of course cannot exist without pitch. Just as dynamics are completely a function of air and embouchure, so it is with pitch. If we change either the air or the embouchure while playing a note, then the pitch will also change. The two parameters of air and embouchure can be changed in four ways. Any of these changes by itself will produce a change in pitch. The four ways are: (1) more air, (2) less air, (3) tightening the embouchure, and (4) loosening the embouchure. For example, if a note is played and then the embouchure is tightened, the note will become sharp. If the embouchure is loosened, it will become flat. If the air is increased, the note will become sharp. If the air is decreased, it will become flat. This is illustrated in Figure 3.

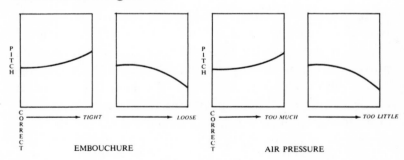

Figure 3.

The player will realize by now that a note is in tune only when a particular quantity of air and a particular embouchure setting are used. Further, these settings must be changed, depending on which dynamic is desired. In remembering what was said before about changing the opening for high notes, we can see that every note on the instrument requires a different setting of air and embouchure, and this is true also for each different dynamic. There are a tremendous number of possible settings on each instrument, and one of the main tasks of the player is to become thoroughly familiar with all of them.

In general, low notes played loud require a loose embouchure with a lot of air, while high notes played soft require a tight embouchure with relatively little air. Figure 4 shows the relationship that exists between the air and the embouchure.

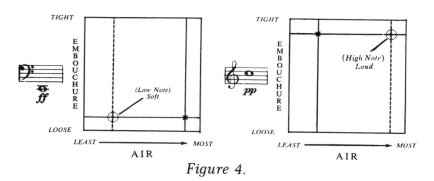

Figure 4.

Crescendo and Diminuendo

For either a crescendo or a diminuendo, we have a dynamic situation during which there is continual change. This change must take place with both the air and the embouchure. Consider a crescendo on middle C, from *ppp* to *fff* (Figure 5).

There is a correct point on the graph for the note at   9 every dynamic between *ppp* and *fff*. When those points are plotted and connected they form a straight line. Any deviation from this (dotted line) would be heard as a change in pitch. In other words, whenever the air or embouchure get out of step with each other, there will be a change in pitch. This may be caused by any of the four variations, that is: too much air, too little air, too tight an embouchure, or too loose an embouchure.

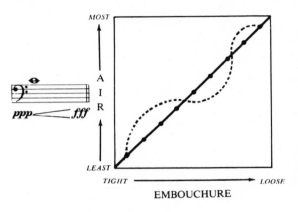

Figure 5.

The diminuendo is the exact opposite of the crescendo, but is more difficult because it is easier to tense a muscle slowly than it is to relax it slowly. Also, minor variations will be more noticeable at low volume than at high because they make up a larger percentage of the whole.

We must learn to blow a stream of air that increases or decreases at a constant rate. This flow of air must not have any bumps in it, nor can it alter its rate of change. At the same time, the embouchure must loosen or tighten at the exact rate to balance the air. This takes a great deal of practice. Doing either well is difficult, but both can only be practiced at the same time, since doing either alone would result in a great change of pitch.

10

Accents

Accents are directly related to dynamics and are produced by exactly the same techniques. There are a number of different kinds of accents, which are written in different ways: >, —, ∧, *sfz*.

The accent alone does not tell us how loudly to play the note. We also need the basic dynamic of the passage. The accent is always somewhat louder than the basic dynamic, and this louder portion of the note is always of a relatively short duration (Figure 6). The exact amount above the basic dynamic is never precisely specified, but the type of accent and our experience with music tell us how much it should be.

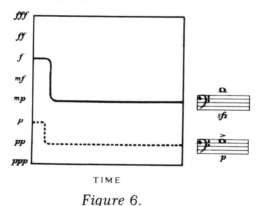

Figure 6.

We can see that the accent consists of a sudden drop in dynamic level to a steady tone. This is difficult to execute because of the sudden change in dynamic, which can only be done by the sudden changing of the air and embouchure. This is in marked contrast to the diminuendo, but is in reality only a diminuendo which is speeded up so as to be almost instantaneous. This is accomplished by starting with a relatively loose embouchure and a large

11

amount of air and then suddenly tightening the embouchure, while at the same time blowing much less air. It is much easier to describe than to perform and requires a great deal of practice. Figure 7 shows the great changes that might be necessary with a strong accent.

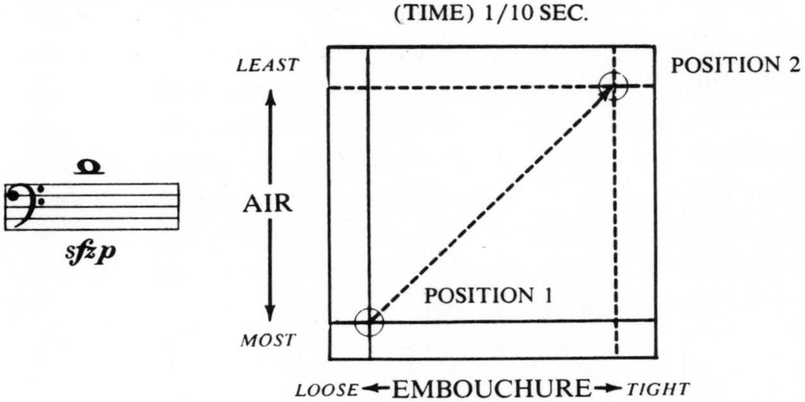

Figure 7.

It is necessary to go from one setting to the other almost instantaneously, and with no change in pitch. A *sfz* on one of the lowest notes would require an even greater change of setting. In order to be able to execute accents properly, we have to know the setting beforehand, because there is not time to hunt for them or to make corrections along the way.

Legato Playing—Connecting Notes

As we play an ascending scale at a fixed dynamic, we notice that the embouchure slightly changes and tightens for each note. Each note has its own setting. The change from one note to the next in a scale is not very great and is fairly easily accomplished. When we are playing intervals or arpeggios, however, the changes are much greater. It is also necessary to make the change of embouchure as quickly as possible, or else we will hear a change in pitch on either the first note or the second. This problem is a little like the one concerning accents, only it is much easier, since there is no volume change involved and therefore relatively little air change. This is one case of the embouchure changing without much change taking place in the air. This fact also makes it easier than the crescendo-diminuendo because we can concentrate on the embouchure while giving relatively little attention to the air.

The pitch of a note in a passage is very much influenced by which note comes before it. Look at Figure 8.

Figure 8.

The F# in the first example results from a sudden tightening of the embouchure from the A. In the second example it results from the sudden loosening from the high E. The two processes are quite different, and a player could easily play the first F# in tune, while playing the second one out of tune. This also happens when one is going to or from a note that is somewhat out of tune on the instrument. The good player has learned how to compensate for the out-of-tune note by changing his embouchure. Therefore, when you go to another note, you must be able to subtract the amount of correction that you had put into the bad note. Again, it comes back to learning the basic setting of air and embouchure for each note, at each dynamic, so

13

that when you play a large skip you can arrive at the second note with the right settings and not have to make audible corrections after the fact.

Exercises

The most important exercise for wind instruments is the "long tone." Long tones are invaluable for learning control of the air and lips—the basis of all playing. In controlling the embouchure and the diaphragm, we employ muscles, which must be brought under a very high degree of control. It takes time to learn to blow an absolutely steady stream of air and to keep the lips from wavering even slightly. This is the only way in which to produce a note with no changes in either pitch or volume.

No activity in everyday life has prepared the diaphragm—which controls breathing—to exhale a steady stream of air for ten or twenty seconds. This is also true of the muscles which shape the embouchure and which must remain in one position while the air is being blown. Any slight fluctuation in either will result in a change in pitch. These fluctuations will be most apparent during the learning process. We should not at first expect to play without them. Only over a period of months will the tone become gradually steadier.

Long tones should be the first exercise in daily practice, but only for 5 or 10 minutes at a time. Stop playing long tones if the lips become too tired. Long tone practicing should not be confined to only a few notes in the range nor to a single dynamic. However, for a while it is best to avoid the extremes of dynamic and range, although eventually these must be practiced as well. Since it is easier to play the louder dynamics, we must spend more time on the more difficult, softer ones which require the lips to be held in a tighter position and which require greater use of the muscles.

After practicing long tones for a few months, the crescendo-diminuendo can then be added. The crescendo-diminuendo is quite different from the straight long tone because the lips-air, instead of being in a steady state, are in a constant state of change. Executing a crescendo requires increasing air, which in turn requires a gradually looser embouchure; thus the lips and air can never remain in one setting. Figure 9 shows the process for a long tone with a crescendo-diminuendo.

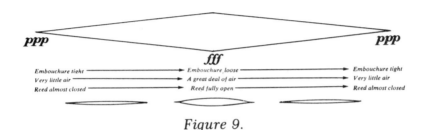

Figure 9.

As we stated before, the accent is related to the diminuendo, but much speeded up. At first, it should be played like a diminuendo, then gradually speeded up. At a certain point, it will begin to sound like an accent rather than a diminuendo (Figure 10).

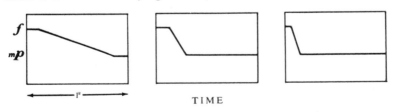

Figure 10.

15

CHAPTER 2

TONGUING, SINGLE AND DOUBLE

The tongue on wind instruments performs the same task as the back-and-forth movement of the bow does on stringed instruments. It is responsible for the articulation of the notes. This is involved with starting and stopping notes of all lengths. One of the difficulties of teaching tonguing is that the entire process is hidden from view inside the mouth. It is not possible for a teacher to demonstrate so that the student can observe the process; neither is it possible to see if the student is doing it correctly.

It is helpful to think of the tongue as a valve that can start or stop the air at will. The natural breathing process is also able to start and stop the air, but it cannot do this with precision and the necessary speed. For this purpose, we need a much greater amount of air—or to put it another way, we need much greater air pressure. We will discuss the basic principles of tonguing first, leaving the subtleties for a later chapter.

The angle and point on the reed at which the tongue

17

strikes is different for the oboe, clarinet, and bassoon. The reason for this is simply the manner in which the instrument is held and the way in which the reed is placed on it. These differences of angle have nothing to do with the basic principles of tonguing, which apply equally to the three instruments.

The ability to use the tongue varies from person to person. There will always be differences in the speed attained by different people, but with practice, everyone can learn to tongue at a satisfactory speed. Very fast single-tonguing is not attainable by all players. However, double-tonguing is, and even a moderately fast double-tongue is faster than the fastest single-tongue. Double-tonguing, therefore, can take care of any lack of speed, and the difference between the fastest double-tonguer and the slowest is rather small, unlike the differences in single-tonguing. Nothing in life has prepared one to tongue on a wind instrument, but learning to speak is a much more complicated process, so there is hope for all beginning wind players.

Staccato

The staccato, or short note, is the most basic kind of tongued note. It is the one from which all the other types of tonguing are derived. This does not mean that it is the most important or the most often used, but that its mechanism is the one from which the others can most easily be derived. The staccato type of tonguing is also the "purest" —no other techniques are involved besides the use of the tongue. This type of tonguing will eventually be used only for fast tonguing.

It is essential that the student realize from the start that this type of short note is nothing more than a fragment of a long note. It is produced in exactly the same way and must have exactly the same tone quality and intonation. There is nothing different about a short note and no special way of tonguing or using the air other than sustaining it. The tongue must not influence the embouchure in any way in the playing of short notes. It must remain independent. If the use of the tongue were to influence the air or embouchure, then inevitably the note would be out of tune, or have some noise component attached to it. Figure 11 demonstrates that a short note is exactly like a long one.

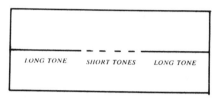

LONG TONE   SHORT TONES   LONG TONE

TIME

Figure 11.

It has been the author's experience that many players who have good tones when they are playing long notes lose this tone when they play short ones. Too many players have come to believe that short notes are expected to sound rough, and therefore apply lesser standards to these notes.

Many otherwise good players attack long notes poorly, as in Figure 12. We can see a great deal of activity (which is difficult to show properly on a simple graph) that lasts only a fraction of a second before settling down to a nice steady tone. This "activity" comes as a result of the wrong setting for the air, the embouchure, or both. The wrong setting may be either the result of a miscalculation or,

19

more likely, of having let the action of the tongue influence the embouchure or air. Any wrong setting will either produce an out-of-tune note or, if it is great enough (which is usually the case in this situation), another note

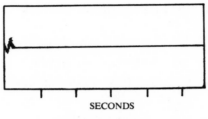

SECONDS

Figure 12.

entirely. Many players start with a setting that is incorrect for any note at all, and therefore are likely to get some kind of "noise" note or a combination note. In any case, the effect is one of roughness on the attack. No player would allow this sound to continue on a long note, and it is corrected very quickly. But what happens to a really short note, one that is no longer than the duration of the roughness? Then we have the typical badly executed short note (Figure 13). When we learn the very specific causes of this roughness, which are in no way mysterious, then we can correct it.

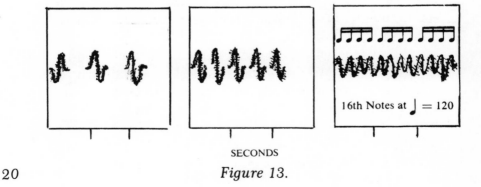

SECONDS

Figure 13.

The Tongue and the Air

When a long note is being properly played, it has a good tone and is in tune. This results from having the right settings of air and embouchure. It is equally important to have the air and embouchure in their proper settings *before* the note is sounded, with the tongue placed on the reed. At this point it is helpful to remember that the tongue acts as a valve to start and stop the flow of air. In other words, the air pressure must be up before the player takes his tongue away from the reed. The tongue is very much like a water faucet, which always has the pressure behind it. The water will flow out as soon as the faucet is opened (Figure 14). The only difference between

Figure 14.

a faucet and the tongue is that a faucet opens gradually, while the tongue moves suddenly. In both cases the pressure is up. In one instance, the height of the water tower and the weight of the water supply the pressure; in the other, the action of the diaphragm and the muscles associated with it supply the air pressure. These muscles press against the lungs, which have been filled with air, and would force the air out if the tongue were not against the reed, closing the valve. The player is going through the

21

motions of blowing, but the tongue will not allow the air out. Then, when the player pulls his tongue back, the air will instantly start to flow. If he has set himself for the right amount of air pressure and the correct embouchure, he will get a "clean" attack.

The pulling back of the tongue requires very little energy and the action should be as relaxed as possible. It should have nothing to do with whether or not the note is played loudly or softly. The tongue must not influence the air or the embouchure. If it does we will hear it as either a noise or a change in pitch or volume. We must strive for the simple act of pulling the tongue back. A steady supply of air and a steady embouchure are essential; otherwise, even if the tongue does its job correctly, we may still have a bad attack. The differences which are felt in the tonguing of a soft note as opposed to a loud one are the result of different degrees of air pressure in the mouth. With very little air pressure, as for a soft note, it is only necessary to place the tongue very lightly against the reed. However, for a loud one this light pressure might allow the reed to start to vibrate, so the player must use a somewhat greater pressure of the tongue against the reed.

After the note has sounded, we will stop it by putting the tongue back on the reed, thus closing the valve and stopping the note. This is done precisely opposite to starting the note, which means that the motion of the tongue must again not influence either the air or the embouchure. We will then be left in the original position, with the air pressure still up. What we have done is to tap the air pressure, which has remained constant, for a brief interval; and since the player is still in the act of blowing, he is ready to start the next note without having lost the pressure. Figure 15 shows the three steps: the start of the note, the sustaining of it, and the stopping of it.

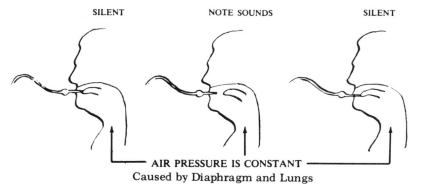

Figure 15.

Most players, it is true, have not learned to tongue in this way. They have started with a type of tonguing which involves movement of the embouchure, and instinctively try to apply this to all types of tonguing. This is a mistake, because we will see that there are several distinctly different types of tonguing which serve different purposes and cannot be mixed. This is why it was stated earlier that this type of short tonguing was the most basic type from which the others are derived, and it must be mastered first. There are two factors that determine how fast a player can tongue. The first one is the actual speed with which an individual's tongue is capable of moving. This is not something that is learned (although one's potential can be developed), but is inherent in the individual. It is partly a matter of reflexes, which vary from person to person. However, the second factor, which is within our individual control, is also important. This is how much distance the tongue travels in performing the operations of tonguing. There is no way to state in fractions of an inch what the ideal distance should be, especially since there is no practical way to measure it. However, the principle is obvious. Suppose the tongue is moving at its fastest speed. Be-

23

tween its most forward position, which is the tip of the reed, and its most backward position, toward the back of the mouth, suppose it moves one inch. In going back and forth, it covers two inches. Moving at the same speed, if it were only to go one-half inch each way, the tonguing would automatically be twice as fast. Therefore, we must learn not to move the tongue more than is absolutely necessary. There is no way to measure the distance that the tongue travels, but we do have a way of gauging it. This is done by listening to how short a note the player can produce. Beginning players usually find it difficult to play very short notes and their goal will be to make them shorter and shorter over a period of many months. One of the main difficulties involves the transition from backward motion to forward motion. Ideally, there should be no pause whatsoever.

First of all, the tongue must move a certain minimum distance from the reed. If this distance is too small there is the danger of the tongue touching the reed by accident. When the tongue reaches the ideal background position, it can either pause or start the return trip immediately. The shortest note will occur when it starts the return trip with absolutely no pause.

We measure the speed of the tongue and the distance it travels by the shortness of the note. Figure 16 shows

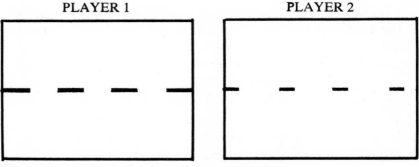

PLAYER 1   PLAYER 2

Figure 16.

two players, each playing the shortest notes he can. They are playing at the same speed. Player 1 can only fit in one other note between beats, while player 2 has time for three or four additional notes. This is why it is of the utmost importance to develop as short notes as possible, because it is the ultimate shortness of the notes that will determine how rapid a staccato a player is to have. No one can tongue faster than the shortest note that he can play.

When we come to the problem of tonguing a series of fast notes, we find that the pause must not only be eliminated at the backward position, but at the forward position as well. The forward position is where the tongue is in contact with the reed. As the player practices staccato, he gradually accelerates the notes until at a particular speed the tongue will be in continuous motion. This speed is the approximate speed of sixteenth notes at a metronome setting of $\downarrow = 120$. The pauses are necessary during the practice period. But we should be aware of them and of the need gradually to eliminate them. The elimination of the pauses, of course, applies particularly to very short notes. The ability to pause is an extremely necessary one when it comes to playing longer notes. Music requires notes of all lengths, from as long as possible to as short as possible.

The type of tonguing that we have been discussing so far only concerns short, or staccato, notes; notes that are meant to be started and stopped with the tongue. There are many other types of tonguing, but before we discuss them, we will go on to a related type that is meant to be used only for very fast notes.

Double-Tonguing

No matter how fast a player is able to single-tongue, there will always be some passages that are either too fast or continue for too long a time. At the same time, there

25

are many players who are excellent in all other ways but who simply do not have a fast single-tongue. The answer to both these problems is double-tonguing. We must realize first of all that double-tonguing is inherently not as perfect as single-tonguing, and therefore it is only meant to be used in fast passages.

Traditionally, flutists and brass players can double-tongue, while reed players cannot. The reasons for this are to be found in the construction of the mouthpiece and its position relative to the mouth. For reed players, the reed is inside the mouth, while for flutes and brass, the mouthpiece is outside the mouth. The tongue of the flute and brass player does not touch the vibrating area, which is beyond the teeth. Double-tonguing is done by first stopping the air with the front of the tongue and then stopping it with the back of the tongue. For reed players there is a tremendous difference between the two. The flutes and brass can stop the flow of air in either the forward or backward position with only a minor difference in sound; they do not have to contend with the positive action of the reed being touched by the tongue.

Think of the way the syllables *ta* and *ka* are formed. The *ta* is formed at the tip of the tongue, while the *ka* is formed at the back. This is the essence of double-tonguing.

We are familiar by now with the *ta* mechanism, since it is the one that is used in starting notes for single-tonguing. In pronouncing the *ka*, we notice that at the moment before actually saying it, the throat is being closed by the back of the tongue. On pronouncing it, the air is suddenly allowed to flow. It is almost as easy to use *ka* to hold back and then start the flow of air as it is to use *ta*. Remember the previous admonition that the pressure is always to remain up during these exercises. The sequence for double-tonguing consists of forming the syllables *takatakatakatakata,* and so on. This is much more easily said than done, partly because of the difference in response between the *ta* and the *ka.*

As in single-tonguing, the player tries to play the notes as short as possible. The first sound, *ta,* must actually end with the back of the tongue in position for the *ka,* but not yet pronouncing it. Then the *ka* is sounded, ending with the tip of the tongue on the reed ready to pronounce the *ta.* The syllables will actually look more like the following: *ta(k)---ka(t)---ta(k)---ta(k),* and so on. The hyphens, ---, represent silence during which the air pressure remains up.

Observant listeners will have noticed that of all the instruments the oboe and bassoon, with the clarinet next, are able to start notes with a clarity and instantaneousness that none of the other sustaining instruments are able to match. This is due to the contact between the tongue and the reed. But as we know it makes the job of matching the *ka* that much more difficult. Figure 17 shows the way in which the *ta* starts, as opposed to the *ka.*

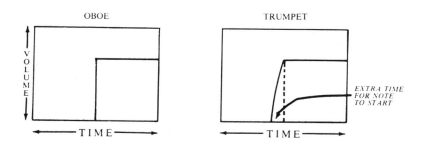

Figure 17.

Obviously, it is simply a matter of time. In Figure 18, the *ta* is shown on the oboe and trumpet. Here we see   27 that the trumpet attack is somewhat like the *ka*, even though the front of the tongue is being used. Thus the brass and flutes have an easier time in matching the *ta* and *ka*.

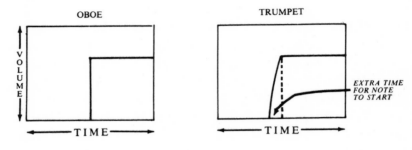

Figure 18.

The actual time differential between the start of the note for oboe and trumpet is extremely small. It is heard not as a time differential, but as a quality of the sound and is in fact one of the ways in which the ear identifies different instruments. Some experiments were made with the AN synthesizer, capable of imitating the sound of any instrument, including its characteristic attack. Two important aspects of the attack are the time it takes and the shape of the slope leading to the fully sustained sound. It was found that if the characteristic attack was taken away and another substituted, it was often difficult or impossible to tell what instrument was playing.

There is another reason for the difference in the time it takes for the sound to start on the reed and nonreed instrument. When the player is set to tongue the reed, the pressure is already in the mouth and therefore on the reed. This can be felt as a sensation in the tongue that the reed is trying to vibrate because of the pressure around it. As the tongue is pulled away, the reed starts to vibrate at once. In contrast to this, as one is set to produce the *ka*, there is no pressure at all on the reed or in the mouth, since it is behind the back of the tongue. Then as the air goes through, it takes a fraction of a second for the pressure to build sufficiently for the reed to start vibrating. This again explains the difference in starting times for the *ta* and *ka*.

In practicing double-tonguing, we must separate the *ta* and *ka* by rather large silences and try to keep pressure up and the embouchure stable; they should not be influenced by the mechanism of double-tonguing. In starting to practice, we will notice the great difference between *ta* and *ka*. The *ta* is very easy to start, but hard to stop, since the stop is done by the back of the tongue. We will also notice that the *ka* is hard to start, while it is very easy to stop it, since the stop is done with the tip of the tongue as it is placed back on the reed. A diagram of the differences is shown in Figure 19.

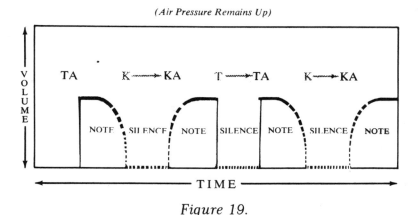

(Air Pressure Remains Up)

Figure 19.

Figure 19 also shows us that the notes tend to have different lengths caused by the slowness of the end of the *ta* as opposed to the quickness of the end of the *ka*. Part of this difference can be attributed to our language training, which is very much ingrained in us. There are many words that start with *ka,* and in these the pressure is automatically built up before we sound the word, but there are relatively few words that end with *ka,* and in these words, we always allow the air pressure to drop drastically as we pronounce them. What we have to do is to train ourselves to stop with *ka* as positively as we do with *ta.*

As in all techniques, we must avoid waste motion at all costs. The player must pull his tongue back only as much as is absolutely necessary in order to pronounce the *ka.* In saying *takatakataka* aloud, we will notice that there is very little waste motion, and that it is done with very little energy. Also we will notice that it is not necessary for the lips to be influenced. The tongue must not transmit any of its motion to them.

The first problem in double-tonguing concerns the lengths of the notes; the second concerns pitch. As we know, any change in either the air pressure or the embouchure, if it is not accompanied by a corresponding change in the other, will produce a change in pitch. Figure 20

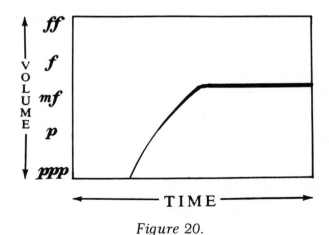

Figure 20.

shows a typically bad *ka* attack. Notice the relatively slow start, which is caused by the time it takes for the back of the tongue to allow the air to enter the reed. The pitch rises with the gradual buildup of air, thus causing the note to be flat as it starts and then quickly go up to pitch. The reason for this is that the player planned his embouchure for a particular amount of air, say *mf*, but this quantity of air only became available gradually because of the relatively slow start of the note. The reverse will be true for a note ending with *ka*. Here the note would tend to become flat. It is not possible to eliminate the gradual buildup of air pressure caused by the *ka*, but it is possible to speed it up to the point where it is not noticed as a buildup. Figure 21 shows three stages in this gradual speeding

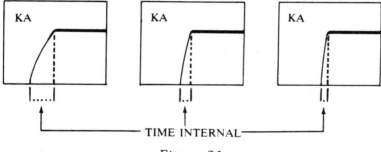

Figure 21.

up of the buildup. By the third example, we have a good sounding *ka*. As in single-tonguing, we will gradually eliminate the pauses between the *ta* and the *ka*, to the point where the tongue is in continuous motion. For single-tonguing, this speed was around sixteenth notes at ♩ = 120. In double-tonguing it is much higher. Figure 22 shows some of the stages in the gradual elimination of the pauses.

Since in double-tonguing the tongue has only about

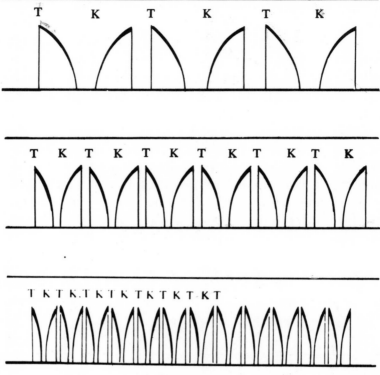

Figure 22.

half the distance to travel as in single-tonguing, it can play almost twice as fast. This ratio is not exactly the same for everyone, but if double-tonguing is practiced properly, a speed of sixteenth notes at ♩ = 180 is easily obtainable. This is fast enough for virtually any example to be found in the literature.

Double-tonguing should not be used in extreme of ranges. The response of the reed is often not quick enough for the highest, and especially the lowest, notes. The reed is always a compromise which favors the most often used part of the playing range. When playing in the extremes of range, one is always using the worst part of the reed's capabilities. Of course, it is entirely possible to build a reed, or have a mouthpiece made, that will favor one of the extremes of range. Indeed, many players change to a special reed when they are faced with solo passages in an extreme range. Fortunately, there are few rapidly tongued passages written in these extreme registers.

Attack and Release of Notes Other than Staccato (Resonance)

Before we explain the different types of single-tonguing, it is necessary to discuss resonance and its application to wind playing. Musicians usually define resonance subjectively, and basically what they mean is that a "resonant" tone is a good tone. This type of resonance takes place during sustained tones. Its qualities are influenced by many factors, some of which are the material from which the instrument is made, its thickness, its shape, the type of reed, the size and shape of the tone holes, and so forth. However, as used in this book the term *resonance* applies specifically to the ends of notes: resonance is prolongation of a sound by reflection or vibration of other bodies. The key words here are "prolongation of sound," for we are interested in seeing what happens to the sound after the written value of the note has passed—that is, the way notes are ended.

Some musical instruments are resonant inherently while others are not. A drum is a perfect example of a resonant instrument. When the drum is struck, the sound starts instantaneously, but does not disappear instantaneously. This natural fading away of the sound is resonance. The amount of time necessary for the sound to die depends on several factors—the size of the drum, how

33

hard it is struck, the stiffness and thickness of the material out of which it is made, the tightness of the skin, and what kind of stick it is struck with. The acoustics of the room also contribute to the length of time which the sound will last, but this is independent of the instrument or player and does not concern us here. Reverberation is the term applied to what happens to a sound as a result of the acoustics of the room.

Figure 23 is a diagram of a single note struck on a drum. Notice that the sound starts instantaneously, as a result of the stick striking the head of the drum. The

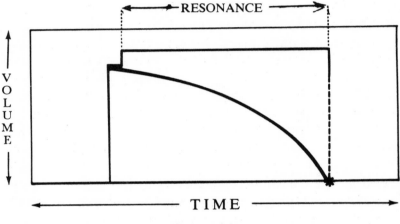

Figure 23.

impetus from the stick disappears almost as soon as the stick bounces off the head. What remains is the gradual decay of the sound. This decaying sound is resonance. It might also be called "natural" resonance because once the player has produced the sound, the amount of time that the tone lasts during its decay is independent of the player. Resonance lasts for a relatively short time, but it is heard very well by the ear. The piano is similarly resonant, but much more so because the sound of its vibrating string is amplified by the large sound board of the instrument. A low note, struck *forte*, will go on vibrating for almost a minute, although for most of this time the sound is extremely soft.

Stringed instruments are also resonant. The vibration of the strings is amplified by the resonant body of the instrument. When the string player lifts the bow at the end of a note, the sound does not die at once. Rather it takes a small, but measurable, amount of time to disappear. This is not the extremely long decay of the piano; it is much shorter and looks like Figure 24. Naturally, a loud note will have a longer resonance time than a soft one.

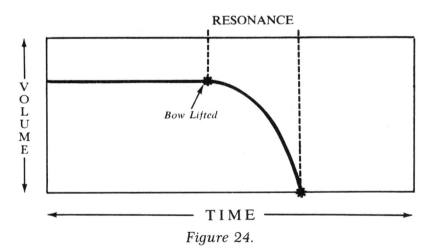

Figure 24.

The only way a string player could cancel out this resonance would be to stop the bow without lifting it from the string, and even then, the stopping of the bow could not be as immediate as is the placing of the tongue back on the reed. String players, however, try to avoid stopping the string except in a few special cases, so that for all practical purposes they always play notes that have resonance. There are very few natural sounds that have no

35

resonance. And in speech the end of a sentence is accompanied by the rapid, but measurable cessation of the flow of air. We are therefore led to the conclusion that sounds which end resonantly are more "natural" and those that end without resonance are less "natural." The exception to this concerns rapid, staccato notes, which come after each other too quickly for us to hear whether or not they are resonant.

The reed instruments by themselves have absolutely no resonance. The bodies of the instruments are purposely made to be stiff and not to vibrate. Thus, when the tongue is applied to the reed, the sound stops instantaneously, there being nothing about the instrument to help keep it going. The brass instruments are only fractionally better because they are much thinner and actually vibrate a very small amount. However, even this is not enough to sound like resonance. Figure 25 shows the relative differences in the endings of notes for piano, violin, and oboe.

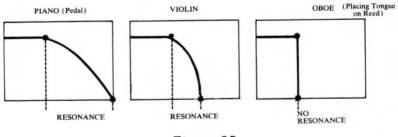

Figure 25.

Remember that the instantaneous ending of notes is necessary and desirable for a rapid staccato, but that now we are concerned with how to give the impression of resonance, where in actuality none exists. Obviously, what we must produce is a graph made by a wind instrument which looks like that of the violin.

In looking at the violin diagram notice that it looks very much like the diagram for a diminuendo. There is, however, a great difference in the time scale. The resonant part of the violin note, for example, lasts but a fraction of a second. A musical note like Figure 26, played on the violin at a moderate tempo, could not possibly have a diminuendo written over it because diminuendos of such short duration are never written.

Figure 26.

Figure 27 shows the difference between a diminuendo and resonance.

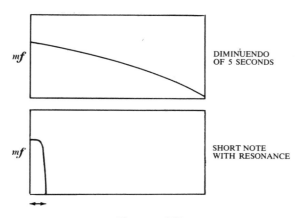

Figure 27.

In making diminuendos of shorter and shorter duration, a point is reached (somewhat less than a half second) where the diminuendo ceases to sound like a diminuendo and starts to sound like resonance. As we will see later, music requires that there be different lengths of resonant endings. Therefore, we will have to learn to play an ending with any amount of resonance that is desired. In the diagrams making up Figure 28, the time scale is very

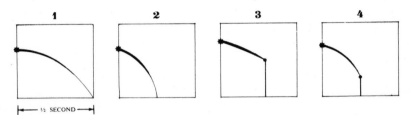

Figure 28.

compressed; each diagram lasts for less than a half second, and shows a different kind of resonant ending. The left side of the diagram indicates where the note would normally stop. That is, if the note were to be played without resonance and ended with the tongue, it would stop at the left margin. In the first two diagrams, we have resonance lasting for different amounts of time. Notice that the note starts to disappear from a particular dynamic, and more or less rapidly goes down to zero. It is very much like a diminuendo, but much quicker. In the next two diagrams, there is a somewhat different situation. Here the same kind of dying away starts to take place, but at a certain point it becomes instantaneous. In example 3, we will hear the cutoff as being too abrupt. In example 4, the sudden cutoff takes place at a soft enough dynamic so that the ear will fill in the missing segment of sound and consequently the cutoff will sound correct. In other words, any abruptness will not be noticed.

Remember that the important thing about resonance is that we cannot hear at what point the note ceases to exist. The rapid dying away of the sound goes down to nothing, and if it is done properly (automatically, on some instruments) we cannot hear the note end.

This is a very important point to remember. Natural resonance always goes down to zero. This is always true unless the player should interrupt it by, for example, going on to the next note before the resonance has been completed. Obviously, as a sound gradually goes down to zero, one cannot hear exactly at what point it ceases. This then is our goal: to be able to produce resonant endings so that the listener, or even the player himself, cannot tell exactly when they end. Figure 29 shows three endings to a note and the relative time scales involved.

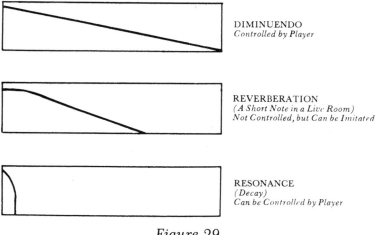

DIMINUENDO
Controlled by Player

REVERBERATION
(A Short Note in a Live Room)
Not Controlled, but Can be Imitated

RESONANCE
(Decay)
Can be Controlled by Player

Figure 29.

A resonant ending on wind instruments is simply an extension of the technique of making a diminuendo. However, it is much more difficult and should not be attempted until the diminuendo is thoroughly understood and mastered. In making a diminuendo, the player has the time to listen to whether or not the pitch is changing, and

39

therefore he can make the necessary adjustments of embouchure or air in order to keep the note in tune. This kind of correcting is not possible with resonance. In other words, the settings must be perfectly correct. Remember that in order to make a diminuendo from *mf* to nothing, it is necessary gradually to blow less and less air, at the same time as we gradually tighten our embouchure. These are the precise operations that take place in playing a resonant ending, except for the speed factor. We must therefore make a rather large change in the embouchure and a large change in the air, all within a fraction of a second. Figures 30 and 31 show some of the typical mistakes made in the execution of resonant endings and the reasons for them.

Figure 30: Failure of the embouchure to close far enough or too fast a decrease of the air. Here we have the

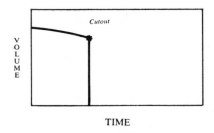

Figure 30.

beginning of the decay, but before it has gone very far there is an abrupt cutoff. The reason is that at that point there was not enough air going through the reed to keep it vibrating. This in itself can have either of two causes. The more common of the two is that the embouchure did not close down far enough. The other, which would produce the same result, is that the air stopped too abruptly. Remember, at this point, that for every opening of the reed, there is a critical amount of air necessary in order for

40

it to vibrate. Any less than that amount will stop its vibrating. As we said before, if the cutoff had occurred at a much later time in the disappearance of the sound, we might not notice it as a cutoff.

Figure 31: The embouchure closes too fast for the air or the air does not decrease enough. The decay rate must always be a constant one. In this case, the rate changes at a certain point which is very apparent to the ear. Again, there are two possible causes resulting in the same effect, and again, it is the first that is much more likely: (1) at the point where the rate changed, the embouchure continued to tighten properly, but the air did not keep pace with it. Instead, it either remained constant, or it slowed down its rate of decrease. The other cause is the opposite of this, namely that (2) the air decreased properly, but the embouchure tightened too fast.

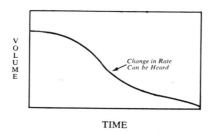

TIME

Figure 31.

These improperly executed endings often result in a pitch change. For example, in the first example, if the change in decay rate had been a little less abrupt, we might have heard the note becoming flat before it disappeared. In the second example, the change in rate of decay would probably be heard as a sharpening of the note. Remember, any mismatching of air and embouchure will result in a pitch change.

So far, we have considered the clean ending of a note

41

and the resonant ending. These are represented in Figure 32. But three other types are still to be considered (Figure 33). Numbers 3 and 4 are very much related to the res-

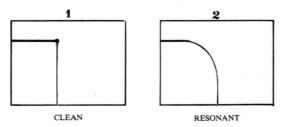

Figure 32.

onant ending because they are merely different lengths of it: (3) short resonance, (4) long resonance, and a fifth type to be considered later.

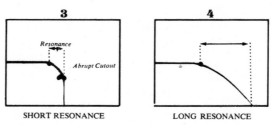

Figure 33.

Notice in particular that the short resonance has an abrupt cutoff near the end of the note. In our previous discussion we mentioned that if the cutoff takes place at a soft enough dynamic, we will not hear it as being abrupt, although we will notice that it produced a shorter note than the resonant or long resonant note. Our goal is to be able to reproduce the three types at will. Their precise uses will be taken up in a later chapter, and a special use for the short resonance will be taken up shortly.

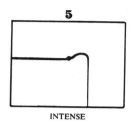

Figure 34.

The fifth type of ending we will call the intense ending (Figure 34). In this ending, there is a short crescendo just before the cutoff, which is of the short resonance variety. The short resonance is meant to occur exactly at the top of the little crescendo. The length of this crescendo will vary considerably depending on the music. It can vary to the extent of virtually being heard as a crescendo, all the way down to only a slight raising of the dynamic level. The resonance always occurs at the *top* of this rise; the energy of the rise is never allowed to dissipate before the resonance starts. In other words, we would not see a diagram like Figure 35, which is incorrect.

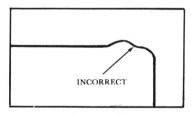

Figure 35.

A Way of Ending Difficult Soft Notes

The better a player becomes, the more aware he is of his limitations and those of his reed and his instrument. For one thing, he knows exactly how softly he can play, 43 and can sense the moment when a note is about to cut out. From this can be developed a technique that can be put to excellent use. At a certain point the note will abruptly cut out. This abruptness can be heard and is not musically pleasant. The top diagram of Figure 36 shows a diminuendo which at a certain point makes an abrupt cutout. This occurs because the player's reed could not play that softly, or because the instrument was not perfectly airtight (which it never is). In any case, it is something beyond the player's control. The cutout is instantaneous, which means that the sound drops suddenly to zero. During a properly produced resonant ending, however, the volume of the note will pass beyond this cutout point on its way to zero. The player could not possibly sustain the note at those soft dynamics, but he is not trying to. The bottom diagram of Figure 36 shows that even though the

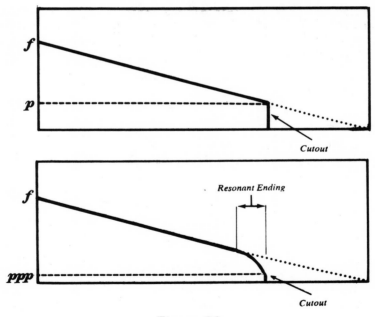

Figure 36.

cutout occurred at exactly the same instant as the first, it was at a much softer dynamic and consequently could not be heard. The player must be able to sense exactly when to apply the resonant ending to the diminishing note. If he allows the note to cut out, but times it properly, he can achieve a much more beautiful result.

Let me restate this, because it is most important to understand it. It is difficult to sustain certain notes very softly or to make extreme diminuendos on them. The danger is that the note will stop suddenly, before the player would have liked. This is not necessarily a lack in the player, but is due to a combination of problems inherent in the construction of the instrument and in reed or mouthpiece inadequacies. Even with the best reed, the cutoff occurs at a certain point when there is too large an opening for the amount of air. As this critical point is reached, the reed will very suddenly stop vibrating, and if this happens at any but the softest dynamics, the ear will perceive it as an unpleasant abruptness. However, when the player senses that the note is about to cut off, he can initiate a resonant ending. This consists of a sudden tightening of the embouchure together with a lessening of the air, causing the note to be much softer before the cutoff actually takes place. What we have done is to close the reed beyond the critical point that was about to be reached, and even though the note couldn't be sustained at those dynamic levels, it does produce a good sounding ending. In other words, the player, during the resonant ending is producing much softer dynamics than he could otherwise play. This technique is difficult, and should not be attempted before the other endings are mastered, but it is well worth learning.

Attacks

CLEAN

In discussing attacks we will not be concerned with endings for the moment, but will consider the attacks as being followed by sustained notes.

Attack has been discussed so far in terms of the proper buildup of air pressure, and the proper embouchure, before the tongue is released. This type of attack is essential for staccato tonguing and is also very important in many other contexts, but it is by no means the only kind of attack we need to learn. However, it is the way to achieve the cleanest attack and is called the clean attack. From this point on we will no longer be discussing staccato, so that the clean attack becomes only one of several types of attack with which we must become familiar. Music has infinite variety and our technique must be capable of expressing this variety.

The clean attack has as its main characteristic the instantaneousness with which it starts. This is represented in Figure 37.

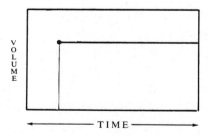

Figure 37.

SOFT

The clean attack, with its primary purpose of clarity, is somewhat similar in its effect to the accent.

The purpose of the accented note is to call attention to itself by standing out from its surroundings. It stands out because the accent itself is of a louder dynamic than the other notes. If we now consider attacking a note which comes after a period of silence, we will see that the "surroundings" of this note, at least on one side, are silence.

The instantaneous attack is therefore somewhat of a surprise, since it is so different from the silence that preceded it. Obviously, in this case an accented note would be even more of a surprise, but we can see that the two kinds of surprise are actually related to each other and only differ quantitatively. An attack on the violin is accomplished by two different motions of the bow arm. One motion is that of bringing the bow down onto the string, and the other is the drawing of the bow across the string, Both contain within themselves a certain element of delay—that is, it takes the string a small amount of time to start vibrating at the desired dynamic. This is partly because it takes the bow a fraction of a second to depress the string to the point where it will produce the desired dynamic. Bringing the bow down on the string with these two motions is not at all like, for example, hitting a nail with a hammer. This would be an instantaneous attack but this is impossible on the strings and would be highly undesirable even if it were possible. A string player could only approach this effect by first placing the bow on the string, then pressing down, and, finally, suddenly starting to draw the bow across the string as quickly as possible. This would result in a very rough, ugly sound, however, and string players try to avoid it. Figure 38 illustrates the

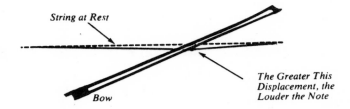

Figure 38.

relationship between dynamics and displacement of the string, and we can see that the displacement must take a certain amount of time to reach.

Remember that these small differences in the time involved in the start of a note are what give each instrument its own characteristic sound. Figure 39 illustrates

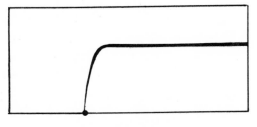

Figure 39.

what actually happens with a string attack. Again, the time scale is very much extended, so that the time needed for the note to rise to the desired dynamic level is but a fraction of a second. Although it is related in its appearance to a crescendo, it in no way sounds like one. Again, it results in a quality of attack which we recognize as belonging to the violin. Notice also that this is very much like the decay in reverse, but is actually quite a bit faster. Figure 40 is a comparison, insofar as time is concerned, between a number of different attacks.

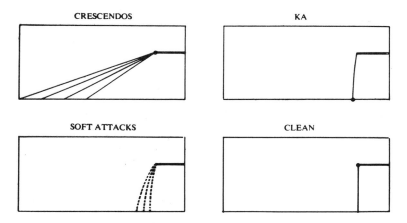

Figure 40.

Notice that at a certain point, just as in the case of the resonant ending, the crescendo ceases to sound like a crescendo and starts to sound like a "soft" attack. As we said before, however, this building up of the dynamic level occurs more quickly than does the decay of a resonant sound. Again going back to nature, we find that sounds generally start much more suddenly than they stop. This is particularly true of the human voice.

The technique for producing a soft attack is the same as that for producing a crescendo, but in an extremely short space of time. Since this space of time is shorter than for the resonant ending, it is harder to learn. One of the keys to proper execution of the soft attack is the ability to start the note softly enough. This again points up the necessity for being able to deal with the extremely soft dynamics: those that fall below the typical *ppp* marking. It is therefore necessary to start the note with the reed quite closed and with hardly any air and then to bring the settings up very quickly to the desired level. Pitch again becomes one of the main problems. This is unlike the string

49

problem because pitch does not enter into the string attack at all. The soft attack is natural to strings and occurs automatically. We are learning to imitate it by understanding the mechanics and reproducing them with the air and the embouchure. In practicing soft attacks, we start with crescendos and gradually accelerate them. Soft attacks are produced much more often in the softer dynamics, but can also occur in loud ones. One of the most difficult problems in the soft attack is that of making the crescendo quick enough and at a steady rate. The most common fault in its execution is to pause at some point in the crescendo, usually at the very beginning. This immediately sounds unnatural, such as the way a bump would in a resonant ending. The "natural" attacks, which are made automatically on some instruments, never have such a bump.

So far three types of attack have been considered (Figure 41).

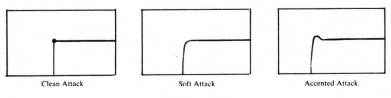

Clean Attack   Soft Attack   Accented Attack

Figure 41.

SFORZANDO AND "EXPRESSIVE"

There are still two types of attack to be dealt with (Figure 42). It is easy to see that the sforzando attack is merely an extreme form of the accent. It is a "hard" accent, or a very big accent. The technique for producing it is only an extension of that used for the accent. A *sfz* always involves at least a forte for the accented part of the

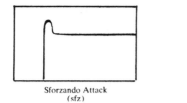

Sforzando Attack
(sfz)

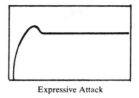

Expressive Attack

Figure 42.

note, unless the dynamic of the passage in which it occurs is a soft one. It is meant to be much more violent than a simple accent. Sometimes, the composer will qualify this marking by requesting more, *sffz* (fortissimo), or somewhat less, *poco sfz* (a little *sfz*).

Notice that the expressive attack is actually a combination of a soft attack and an accent. Its purpose is to bring out the note, but in such a way as to minimize the surprise or suddenness of the attack. It makes the note stand out, but without the violence of an accent. It is clear that it should take much longer than the soft attack or the accent. However, it still must not sound like a crescendo, although it tends toward it, and the end of it must not sound like a diminuendo. In Classical and Romantic music, the expressive accent was usually indicated by *fp*. Figure 43 gives an idea of the way it would look and shows how the diminuendo and the crescendo would be quite different in timing.

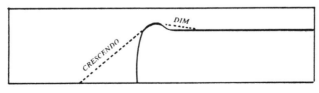

Figure 43.

51

The attacks and releases dealt with vary in difficulty. They should not all be learned at the same time because the more difficult ones depend for proper execution on the prior mastering of the easier ones. Beyond this, it is necessary first to have a thorough understanding, together with the ability to execute them, of the techniques of crescendo and diminuendo before attempting the various attacks and releases.

Exercises

SINGLE-TONGUING

These are not to be confused with exercises for the various kinds of attacks; they are only for the purpose of attaining a fast staccato, and are concerned mainly with the shortness of individual notes. Figure 44 gives the basic form of the exercise.

As we can see, the exercise is to be combined with the playing of long tones. This is absolutely essential because the short notes must be exactly like the long tone in quality and in pitch. Combining them in the same exercise will allow us to compare them constantly. During this exercise, the air pressure must remain up between notes and at the same time the embouchure setting must be as fixed as possible. One reason for taking plenty of time between notes is that we can then have time to be aware of the settings. The exercise is performed on the notes of a scale (that is, after each note is first repeated and then held) at first avoiding the extremes of register, then gradually introducing them.

The ideal way to play the exercise is illustrated in Figure 44. However, this is not the way it will be at the

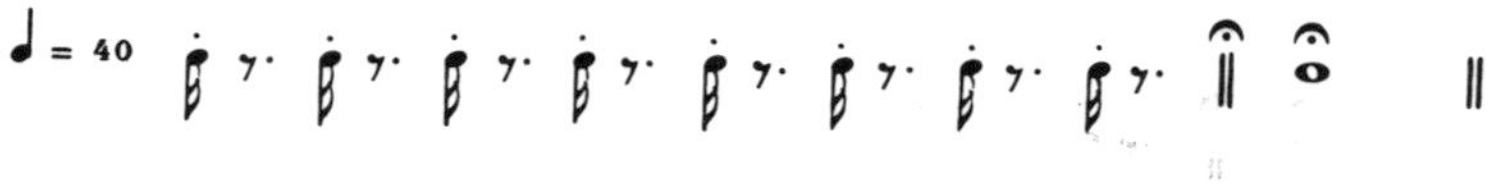

Figure 44.

beginning. Instead it may look like Figure 45. This is perfectly correct. The reason for it is that when the player hears the short note sounding badly, he should immediately play the long one, which will show him where his settings have gone wrong. At the beginning the settings will inevitably wander away from the correct ones; therefore

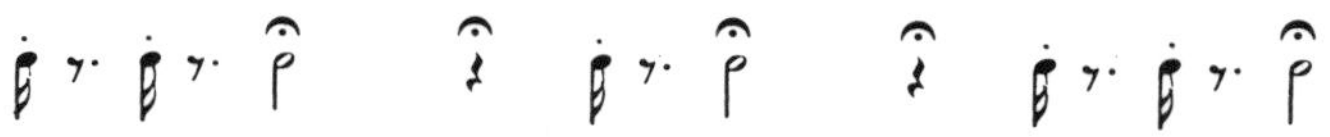

Figure 45.

we need the long tone to set us right. Remember, during the playing of a short note, there is no time to make corrections. In the beginning the player will not notice that the short notes are sounding badly. The only way to remind himself of this fact is to intersperse the short notes with the longer tones. This is not for the long tone exercise itself, but only to compare the pitch and quality of the short notes with the longer ones. Remember, it is the long tones that will undoubtedly show where the correct settings are. We strive to apply these to the short notes without letting the settings change. The crux of the matter is to be able to play the staccato notes while the settings remain fixed; that is, without letting the act of tonguing influence them. Then when we are sure of tonguing without modifying the settings, we can begin to speed up the repititions of the short notes.

Over a period of months, the speed is gradually in-

53

creased until we reach ♩ = 100. Then the exercise is changed to the pattern shown in Figure 46. The object in playing the group of four sixteenths is to keep the tongue relaxed and light. The distance which the tongue moves should be kept to a minimum. We are aiming toward a goal of ♩ = 120, and being able to play sixteenth notes at this speed.

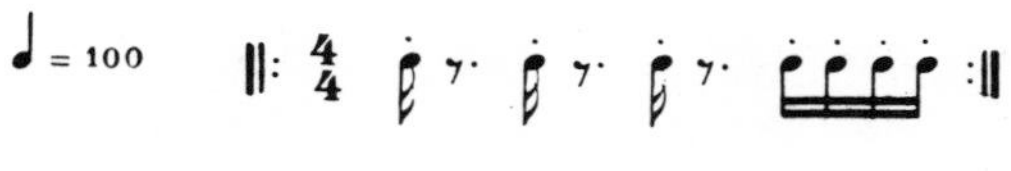

Figure 46.

DOUBLE-TONGUING

Double-tonguing should not be started until the single-tongue is well under control, which will probably be from six months to a year. As we said before, one of the main concerns in double-tonguing is to match the lengths of the *ta* and *ka*. This is to be done very slowly at first, as in Figure 47. Over a period of months the speed is to be increased. When it has become somewhat stabilized, it will be helpful to start the exercise with the *ka* rather than the *ta*. This will help make the *ka* stronger, since it is on

♩ = 40

Ta   Ka   Ta   Ka

Figure 47.

the downbeat. Another variation is to practice only *ka*s: *ka(k)---ka(k)---ka(k)---ka(k)*. When the speed has advanced to about ♩ = 120, the sixteenth notes should be put into a scale, starting with *ta*s and *ka*s.

Many examples of fast tonguing passages begin as in Figure 48. Obviously this should be started with the *ka*. Until recently, brass and flute players used triple tonguing when playing fast triplets. But triple tonguing is not possi-

Figure 48.

ble on the reed instruments, and it has been found that even on triplets, double-tonguing sounds more even (Figure 49).

Ta Ka Ta Ka Ta Ka Ta Ka Ta

Figure 49.

Combinations Of Attacks And Releases

The five types of attack are:
(1) Clean; (2) Soft; (3) Accented; (4) Strong Accent *(sfz)*; and (5) Expressive.

The five types of release are:
(1) Clean; (2) Resonant; (3) Short Resonant; (4) Long Resonant; and (5) Intense. The clean attack and the clean release were discussed in the section on staccato. The other attacks and releases can be practiced in combination

55

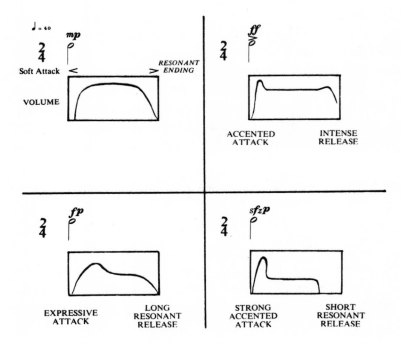

Figure 50.

with each other. Some examples are shown in Figure 50. Any combination is possible, and all should be practiced. As we can see, there are twenty-five possibilities. It is important in the beginning to leave plenty of time after the attack and before the release so that there is enough time to concentrate on each properly.

CHAPTER 3

VIBRATO

*T*here are basic disagreements about vibrato between the different schools of wind playing and even between individuals of the same school. One of the reasons for this difference of opinion is that vibrato is still relatively new for the wind instruments. Another is that there are at least three entirely different ways of producing a vibrato on a wind instrument. Because vibrato is relatively new, we find that many of the older players do not use it and therefore do not teach it to their students. There is also a tradition against the use of vibrato for the clarinet and the French horn. This tradition is definitely changing, but those clarinetists and French horn players who use it are still very much in the minority. Whether or not vibrato should be used on the horn and clarinet is strictly a matter of opinion, and the author will not get involved in that discussion. However, the vibrato to be discussed could be used on any of the wind instruments.

Vibrato is a regular pulsation in the sound, brought about by either a change in pitch or a change in volume.

As with the diaphragm vibrato, there can also be a change in both. We can actually see a vibrato in action by observing string players. We see it as a back-and-forth motion of the left hand, and it is easy to understand how it produces a change in pitch. The amount of pitch change varies from person to person and from musical situation to musical situation, but the pitch variation must always be less than a half step; otherwise it would sound like two different notes being played. This kind of vibrato is the only one available to the strings. The winds, however, must choose between three types:

1. Diaphragm (and the associated muscles). These are the muscles that control breathing.
2. Lip, or embouchure. This is executed by moving the lower jaw up and down.
3. Throat. This is executed with the very back of the tongue against the throat. It is somewhat like a constant repetition of the word "ah," without the use of the voice, and with a definite closing of the throat at the end of each "ah."

The trombone is the only wind instrument that can produce precisely the same type of vibrato as the strings. This is done by moving the slide in an out, thus changing the pitch in the same way as the strings. Some trumpet players achieve a vibrato by actually shaking the instrument with their hands. This results in the embouchure setting being periodically altered and thus causing a pitch change. This is in a sense the most primitive way of producing a vibrato, and it is surprising to hear how far it can be refined. Usually, though, it is somewhat uneven and lacks the subtleties attainable by some of the other methods.

Singers, who by a slight stretch of the imagination can be considered wind instruments, use the diaphragm vibrato. This is not true of all singers, but it is true of singers of Classical music. In watching a singer, notice that the throat seems to pulsate and in some cases, even the mouth as well. This results from the air pulsations produced by the diaphragm. In other words, these movements of the throat and mouth are after-effects of the changes in pressure caused by the diaphragm and are not in themselves a cause of the vibrato. Experience has proved to the author that the diaphragm vibrato is far superior to any of the other types. Such a preference, however, cannot be sustained with scientific proof, it is a matter of personal preferences. At this time, this belief is very strongly held, and to the author represents a "truth." For that reason, diaphragm vibrato will be the only type to be discussed.

Diaphragm vibrato is produced by the same set of muscles (which for simplicity's sake will be called the diaphragm) that is responsible for breathing in and out. These are, of course, the same muscles that allow us to blow a steady stream of air. In vibrato, however, there should not be an absolutely steady stream of air, but rather a series of pulsations that are imposed onto a steady stream. (A word of caution: before vibrato is attempted, the player must first be able to play absolutely steady long tones. This kind of firm base is necessary before trying to alter the steady base by putting a vibrato on top of it.) The pulsation is a sudden burst of air. If we imagine blowing out a match, we will have the impression of a rather large and sudden burst of air. Notice that it increases to its maximum very quickly and then just as quickly decreases. It would look like Figure 51.

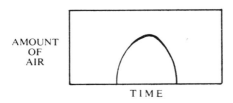

Figure 51.

The Basic Pulse

If desired, we could control the slope up as well as the slope down in order to make it more gradual. This is the basic mechanism for vibrato, with one important difference. The vibrato pulse does not come from zero, nor does it return to zero, because zero represents silence. Vibrato is always placed on an already existing stream of air. The diagram for a single pulse, then, would look like Figure 52. The straight line represents the note at a steady

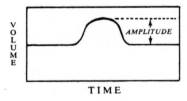

Figure 52.

mp level, and the upward curving line represents an increase in volume, followed by a similar decrease in volume. The word amplitude is used to describe the amount of difference between the base dynamic level and the top of the curve. At this point remember one of our basic rules: any change in the air without a corresponding change in the embouchure will produce a change in pitch—a situation to avoid at all costs. Here, however, this change in pitch is actually desirable because it is one of the two ingredients of vibrato. In other words, during the sudden bursts of air, which are the vibrato pulses, there is no thought given to trying to change the embouchure, and the result is a change in pitch as well as a change in volume. The change in pitch tends toward making the note sharper. We could produce a vibrato in which the note became flatter instead, but this sounds worse and should be avoided. With the flatter note, the volume would go down instead of up; another situation which will not sound well.

If we look again at the vibrato pulse, we will notice the similarity with the crescendo and diminuendo, which we also noticed in discussing soft attacks and resonant releases. Just as in those cases, the time scale is quite different. Vibrato pulses are meant to be quick enough so that they do not sound at all like crescendo and diminuendo. The speed of the pulses on wind instruments varies from about four to six or seven per second.

Common Faults

In practicing vibrato we are at first interested in only one pulse at a time. Our object is to have the pulse take place as quickly as possible, both up and down. Figure 53 shows three typical mistakes made in practicing the pulses.

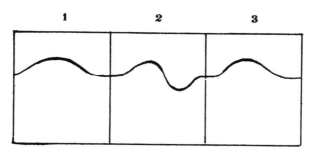

Figure 53.

In Example 1, the rise and fall take place too slowly.
In Example 2, instead of returning to the original dynamic level, the note first becomes too soft.

61

In Example 3 is the most common mistake: the rise is done correctly, but the fall takes place too slowly.

In Example 3, when the player tries to speed up the pulsations—that is, to have them come closer together—he will find that there will not be enough time to get the note back down to the original level before it is time to start the next upward pulse. This will result in a very narrow vibrato and one which will make the note sound sharp (Figure 54). The quicker the up and down of the pulse, the more pulses we will eventually be able to fit in a second.

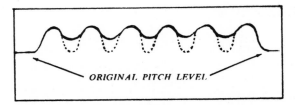

Figure 54.

In practice, we find that the push up is easier to achieve than the dropping down. To accomplish this it is necessary to stop the pushing impulse as soon as it is started, instead of, as it were, riding up the crest and then riding down. The only control exercised in riding down is to be sure that we get back to the original dynamic level. It is not necessary to control it beyond that. During the practice period we find that as we gradually speed up the recurrence of the pulses, there will come a point—around four per second—where it is no longer possible to pause between the pulses. There is a similarity in this between practicing vibrato and practicing short notes for staccato (Figure 55).

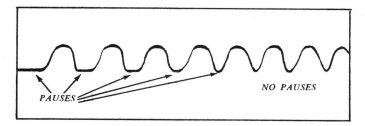

Figure 55.

Variables to Be Controlled

There are several variables in the use of vibrato which must be dealt with, such as the speed of the pulses (number of times per second) and the amplitude of the pulses.

Another variable concerns the starting and stopping of the vibrato; that is, gradual starting or stopping as opposed to sudden starting and stopping. This will be discussed later on.

The speed of the pulses varies from about four per second to seven per second. This entire range of pulse rates, however, does not apply to all the winds; rather it is the overall range from faster vibrato of the flute to slower vibrato of the bassoon. Of the factors determining which speed to use, the most important is the music itself. That is, whether or not it is emotional or placid. Beyond this there is the question of which range of the instrument is being used. The lower range of any given instrument should have a slower vibrato than the upper range, and at the same time this slower rate must have a wider amplitude. One of the main reasons for this is that the notes are farther apart in the lower range than in the upper. We can see this by looking at the frets of a guitar. The higher we ascend into the upper register, the closer together they become. If a string player were to use as wide a vibrato in the upper register as he does in the lower, he might find himself covering more than the range of a semitone. In general the violin and the flute have a faster, narrower vibrato than do the cello and the bassoon.

The greater the amplitude of the vibrato, the more noticeable it is in calling attention to itself. At a certain point, however, it ceases to sound like vibrato and will disturb the listener. This is sometimes called a wobble in the tone. The opposite of this is the too narrow vibrato, one with a very small amplitude. This tends to make the tone less noticeable, until it could become bland and uninteresting. The player must be able to use all the different degrees of amplitude as well as the different speeds. In Figure 56, we might call (1) normal, (2) intense, (3) peaceful, and (4) cold or bland.

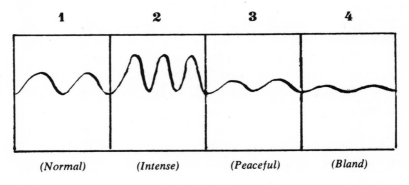

<table>
<tr><td>1</td><td>2</td><td>3</td><td>4</td></tr>
</table>

(Normal) *(Intense)* *(Peaceful)* *(Bland)*

Figure 56.

It was mentioned before that one of the variables in the use of vibrato concerned starting and stopping it. In starting it, the most basic way is to have the vibrato begin together with the note. This is the method most often used. Until the player masters the immediate starting of the vibrato, he should not go on to some of the different ways of starting it. One factor that makes the immediate starting of the vibrato difficult is that the start of the note and the start of the vibrato are both executed by the same mechanism; that is, the diaphragm. What is happening is that while the diaphragm is expelling the air in a continuous stream, it is at the same time pulsating to produce the vibrato. When we start a note with vibrato, we must be able to start the pulsing at the same time as the note. Otherwise there will always be a delay before we hear the vibrato. As we will see shortly, such a delay can be an important expressive device, but it must be under the control of the player; otherwise it will always take place whether or not it is appropriate to the music.

When the immediate starting of the vibrato is mastered, the student can proceed to some of the other types as pictured in Figure 57:

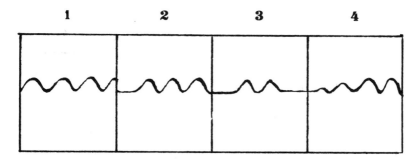

Figure 57.

1. A steady vibrato.
2. The vibrato starts after the note starts.
3. The vibrato starts after the note starts and ends before the note ends.
4. The vibrato starts gradually.

When to use each of the different types will be taken

65

up in a later chapter. Always remember that vibrato is not meant to be used automatically, as the vibrato stop is used on an electric organ. This nullifies its effectiveness and makes all expressiveness of an equal kind, a practice that goes against the very grain of music. It is also important to remember that not every note of every piece requires the use of vibrato. There are some players who use it all the time. Besides destroying expressiveness, there can be another serious consequence. Consider Figure 58, in

Figure 58.

which we have a moderately fast scale, to be played legato. When the player uses vibrato while playing the scale, the speed of the pulses of the vibrato is similar to the speed of the notes themselves. In actual practice, it is not possible to keep these two exactly synchronized, and they would probably be going in and out of phase. Remember that the vibrato is also a change in volume. We can see that the notes at the peak point of each pulse will sound a little louder than the other notes, while those at the lowest point would sound softer. All this has the effect of making the scale sound somewhat nonlegato, often quite contrary to the intention of the composer. The result would be rather like that if the composer's marking were marcato (marked, or somewhat accented) on each note. This effect would not be noticeable if the scale and the speed of the vibrato pulses were far apart. However, the average speed of a vibrato happens to coincide with some of the most often used speeds of sixteenth notes. The point is not to use the vibrato automatically, but to use it always for a musical reason.

Exercises

BEGINNING VIBRATO

Begin at a pulse speed of ♩ = 60 (Figure 59). Gradually increase over a period of six months to a year to a pulse speed of from four to seven per second, depending on the instrument and the musical passage. Seven is extreme and does not apply to the bassoon. Four is also extreme and does not apply to the flute or oboe. From five to six per second is the normal pulse range.

Figure 59.

INTERMEDIATE VIBRATO

Up to this point it has been necessary to count pulses with each note. However, when the vibrato is well under control, but not yet at the proper rate of speed, we must begin to eliminate the counting process. This is not as easy as it sounds. With our first attempt, we find that evenness disappears or the amplitude has become very narrow. Do not try to overcome this too hurriedly; this is a necessary phase to go through. Try to play scales slowly and change the notes at random. In this way we can be-

67

gin to separate the pulses from the rhythm of the notes. Another technique to master at this point is the ability to begin notes with the vibrato coinciding with the start of the note. Think of the note starting at the top of the first vibrato pulse.

ADVANCED VIBRATO

At this stage we should be able:
1. To start notes with and without vibrato.
2. To change the speed of the pulses while playing.
3. To use vibrato at extreme dynamics.
4. To change the amplitude while playing.

CHAPTER 4

TECHNIQUE

The term "technique" is used here to apply specifically to the fingers. Assuming that the player has learned the correct fingering for every note on his instrument, we will then be concerned with the mechanical operations necessary in changing from one fingering to another. It may be helpful first to examine the ways of opening and closing holes on the woodwinds:

1. Putting a finger, or fingers down on an open hole, to close it.
2. Lifting fingers from an open hole, to open it.
3. Pressing a key down, to close a hole; also lifting a key to close it.
4. Pressing a key down, to open a hole; also lifting a key to open it.

The problem of moving only one finger on a key or a hole is relatively simple and rarely causes difficulties. However, when we have to deal with all the possible combinations of the fingers, changing in rapid succession, the situation becomes quite complicated.

Let us first consider the difference between open holes and keys. We are dealing in purely mechanical terms involving distance, time, and leverage. Obviously, in these terms (open holes and keys) two situations exist. Most bassoons have five completely open holes, clarinets have seven, and oboes and flutes have none, although some student oboes do have a few. There is no question of leverage, resistance, or distance from the open holes; it is simply a matter of the finger coming down to close the hole. With keys, the situation is very different. In the first place, they are not of uniform length, although the flute keys are closer to each other than any of the others. Keys were invented in response to the need for better intonation and greater range, which meant locating holes at points on

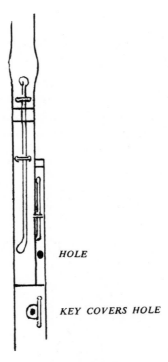

HOLE

KEY COVERS HOLE

Figure 60.

the instruments that the fingers could not reach. It was also found to facilitate technique if some of the newly invented keys could be made to open or close more than one hole at a time. Figure 60 shows three keys on the bassoon. Note the great difference in length.

In examining the various woodwinds, notice that the keys are mounted so that they move in quite a few different ways. Some move perpendicular to the instrument, some at different angles, and some turn as they move; it is also necessary to slide from one key, which has been pressed, to another which is also meant to be pressed. Besides some of these built-in differences, it is necessary to play keys with entirely different parts of the finger itself (Figure 61).

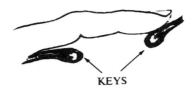

KEYS

Figure 61.

On the bassoon it is sometimes necessary to press three or four keys with one finger. Since one of the secrets of a good technique is the exact synchronization of all the different finger motions, we can appreciate the difficulty of the situation.

Consider Figure 62, which illustrates one aspect of finger technique. The first note is played with finger A down on its hole. The next note has finger A lifted, and finger B put down on its hole. If finger A were to come off the hole before finger B goes down, then this interim fingering—that is, with no holes covered—would produce another note. Further, if B goes down before A comes up, then we have still another note. It is impossible for even

71

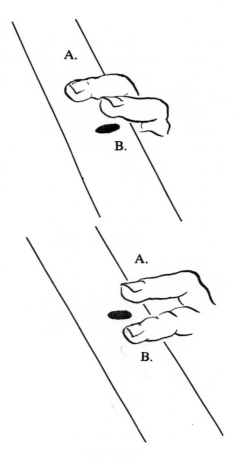

Figure 62.

an expert player to change from one fingering to the other without some overlap. However (and this is the crux of the matter), when this operation is carried out properly and *with the necessary speed,* it becomes impossible to hear the extra note because it lasts for much too short a time. The obvious conclusion is that for the proper execution of finger changes, it is essential that they be carried out with perfect synchronization and with the greatest speed possible. The principle to bear in mind is that once the fingering change has been decided upon, it must be executed in a rapid, positive manner. The absolute speed with which a player is able to move his fingers will determine the upper limits of his technique. This is not to say that we can simply rely on fast reflexes. The potential about which we have been speaking is realized only with the proper practice. Virtually everyone has the potential to play most of the technical passages called for, but it remains for those few with the greatest potential to become virtuosos.

The most important consideration, with the exception of absolute speed, is the distance that the fingers have to move. This is very much like the situation with regard to tonguing—the less distance to be covered, the better. However, there are two important factors concerning how little one can lift the finger. One is that if the finger is kept too close to a hole, the note will be made flat or will sound muffled. The other is that the keys must be solidly and somewhat forcibly closed, otherwise they could permit air to leak out. We must therefore find that point above the keys which allows for the least movement consistent with the proper closing of the holes. Figure 63 shows what happens as a key is closed:

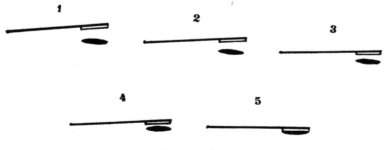

Figure 63.

73

1. The key is completely open, and the note sounds properly.
2. The key is partially closed, and the note still sounds properly.
3. At some point between 2 and 3, the note will start to become flat; the closer it gets to 4, the flatter it gets.
4. The note now starts to become more and more choked, besides being very flat. At a point just before it is fully closed, the note may cut out altogether.
5. The key is fully closed, and the next note sounds properly.

There is no way to avoid this sequence of events, and it makes no difference whether it is a key or an open hole. The only remedy is speed. As was said before, if the sequence takes place quickly enough, then no one would hear anything but a perfect change.

Playing Difficult Passages

In the first part of this chapter we have discussed the mechanics of finger movements and the necessity of avoiding waste motion, which is central to the efficient realization of any task. We can tolerate waste motion if we are speaking of a modest amount of speed, but in every field of human endeavor, especially in athletics and in the performing arts, the concept of what is possible is always being pushed to the limit. It is here that differences in reflexes and in efficiency are critical. Many fast passages in music approach the borderline of what is possible, and any bad habits which might have been overlooked in slower passages will now show up only too clearly.

The change from one note to the next could involve

as many as nine or ten fingers, or any combination of these. Because of these different combinations, some changes are far more difficult than others, and yet the amount of time allowed for each change is exactly the same. This would be typical in a fast sixteenth-note passage. (Some problems that appear to be caused by poor finger technique are actually caused by poor control of the air and embouchure. These problems will be discussed later.)

In the execution of a difficult passage, there are two distinctly different problems. One concerns the ability to play any of the combinations perfectly, in isolation; that is, the ability to make the change from one note to another with perfect synchronization. The problem of synchronization is one which we have discussed before. If every change of fingering were to be executed perfectly, then the second problem would never arise. But this is very often not the case, even when a player can handle any two notes at a time. In other words, playing many different combinations in rapid succession introduces a factor not found in any two-note combination, and the player wonders why he cannot play the whole passage when he can play individually each combination perfectly.

Figure 64 shows a bassoon passage from Ravel's *Bolero,* and has some very difficult fingering changes in it. The numbers placed between each two notes represent the relative difficulty of each change; 1 is the easiest and 10 the most difficult.

Figure 64.

75

Notice that the degree of difficulty is constantly changing. Consider what happens when we play a combination of three notes, with relative difficulties of 9-4. In other words, between the first and second notes, there is a difficulty of 9 (quite difficult), and between the second and third notes, a difficulty of 4 (fairly easy). What can happen is that while difficulty is expected with the 9, the 4 will also cause trouble. The reason for this is that the synchronization problems of the 9 have resulted in the fingers not all being in their correct positions relative to the second note before it is time for them to move to the next position, the one for the third note. Some of the fingers will have had an easier task than others and will be in the correct position. (Of course all the fingers do not move with the same sureness; fingerings involving the fourth finger always cause more trouble.) If some of the fingers do lag, they will be late not only for the first change, but also for the second. They do not skip an operation, they simply perform it more slowly. On a simple two-note change, even if there is some delay, the second note will sound correctly, because the lag is rarely for more than a fraction of a second. However, in a rapid passage, no single note may last for more than a fraction of a second. We find, therefore, that a difficult combination influences other fingerings beyond itself. It can actually take the fingers a number of notes to "settle down" after a difficult combination. No note is an absolute entity by itself; rather the difficulty depends on which note is before it and which note is after it. This means that the same note which was fairly easy in many combinations can become very difficult in others. In other words, the problems in a dynamic situation are quite different from those in what we might call a static situation; that is, one in which there are only two notes involved.

In the final analysis, it is simply a matter of speed of

finger movement. This cannot be denied; but even within each person's potential, there is much that can be done to improve the situation. Foremost is the ability to concentrate. Consider the following statement: something is not completely learned until one can do it without having to concentrate. This may at first seem to be a contradictory statement. What it means is that the performing of an operation by habit is always smoother than one done with concentration. The act of concentrating, which takes quite a bit of energy, deprives the muscles of some of their speed. It puts controls on them. Concentration takes a certain amount of time, the kind of time that does not exist in a fast passage. Concentration is of the utmost importance in the learning process, but at a certain point it can become a hindrance. We have to learn to be able to bring our concentration to bear on exactly that point in the passage where it is needed, and in no other place. Also there might be several different places in one passage where we will have to concentrate. The ability to focus all our concentration on one place can be developed, but it takes will power.

Important as the ability to concentrate is, we must first know precisely where to concentrate, we must know exactly what is wrong with a particular passage. This is not as easy as it may sound. The difficulties are not apparent when the passage is played slowly, or if they are, they are often of a different nature. We must listen to the passage played in tempo and be able to tell exactly what is wrong. Our ear must be trained to analyze very quickly, because the notes are being played so fast. The ear must hear only the problem note or notes and not the one before or the one after. Otherwise, we can spend hours working on a particular passage without improving it, but ten minutes of the right kind of work will master it.

In a passage where three notes in a row are badly

executed, we must first find the exact point where the difficulty starts. It is at this point that we must first direct our concentration. It may be necessary first to play the passage many times, at about the right tempo, until we can readily identify the exact spot. When we feel that we know this is it, we then play the passage again, right up to the trouble spot. At this point, the last note is held. During the time that this note is to be held—which should be for several seconds—the concentration is brought to bear on the fingering of that note and, more especially, on the next note. We must get the feeling of what the next fingering is to be. This change is then made as quickly and positively as possible, with the fingers "clicking" into place with all possible definiteness. Only when this concentration has been focused and the player feels sure of the next change, will he then go on and finish the passage. This is to be done several times, with a real pause for regrouping of the thoughts before the passage is tried with no pause (as written).

Figure 65 shows what could be a difficult passage, and the way to practice it. After this passage has been practiced in the manner shown, it should then be played straight through, in tempo. At this point, we may be sur-

Figure 65.

78

prised to find that there are now other spots in the passage which we did not notice before that are being played poorly. This could happen as a result of the original difficult passage having covered up some of these less difficult ones of which we were unaware. Another reason for this new difficulty is that, after mastering the first difficult passage, we find the fingers in a different position. We then have to work on these new difficulties in exactly the same way as on the first. They are taken in order and worked on one at a time, so that the next step may involve playing the passage as shown in Figure 66.

Figure 66.

During the practicing of the newer problem, we may find that we are again losing what we have gained on the first one. If that happens—and it is likely—then we must return to the first one again. Such are the problems of conquering a difficult passage.

Embouchure and Air

The embouchure-air settings can be as much a problem in a technical passage as the fingers. Such problems often arise when skips are involved rather than scalelike passages. All notes on the instrument do not respond in the same way to fast legato slurs. This is because some notes, in terms of the acoustical structure of the instru-

79

ment, are like certain other notes, either because they have similar fingerings, or because one note may be a harmonic of another note. When one of these is the case, slurring between the two notes is more difficult. In other words, the second note must have additional help if it is to respond quickly enough. This becomes especially difficult in a fast passage. One way of correcting this problem is in the use of special slur fingerings, which are different from the normal ones. These slur fingerings help the second note to "speak" precisely because they are less like the original note. Special fingerings will be taken up again later, but for the present our concern is with the correction brought about by the air, or embouchure, which is especially important because special fingerings do not exist for all the difficult slurs.

In a difficult fingering change, we noted that it was necessary to make the change as quickly as possible and with a positive action. This also applies to changes for the embouchure and the air. The time for such changes is as limited as it is for the fingers, and must take place just as quickly as the fingers. But as was discussed, even a perfectly correct change of air-embouchure may not produce the slur. It may be necessary to overcompensate for the difficult slur. One way of doing this is with a technique that would produce an accent on the second note. In slurs that go up, it helps to have a momentary embouchure setting for a higher note than the one in question. Conversely, in slurring down, it helps to set the embouchure momentarily for a lower note than the difficult one. Of course, the embouchure must be brought back as soon as the note has started to sound. Any delay in doing this will produce an audible change in pitch. Therefore, in practicing fast passages, it is most important to know if the difficulties are being caused by fingering problems or by air-embouchure problems. Unfortunately, both problems are often present. Unless they are separated and analyzed, there is little chance of correcting them.

Although it is important for the embouchure to be able to change as definitely as the fingers, in actual practice this is not possible. We try to achieve it, but the embouchure-air cannot "click" into place the way the fingers can. This becomes especially apparent in an arpeggio where there are only skips. During the arpeggio, the embouchure is in continuous motion and follows the shape of the arpeggio, either up or down. This means that it is in a constant state of either getting tighter or looser. The final note of the group is the one that the embouchure must aim for, although with practice it is possible to be correct at most points. This is also true for the air, which always works with the embouchure. Figure 67 shows an arpeggio and the sweep of air-and embouchure that must accompany it.

Figure 67.

There is a perfectly correct and definite setting for only two points on the arpeggio; the first note and the last. Therefore, the player must gauge the speed of the arpeggio, so that he will make the necessary changes in time to arrive perfectly with the last note. One of the common faults in playing an arpeggiated figure is to have the tight embouchure that will be needed for the last high note one

81

or two notes too early. These two notes will then sound pinched and sharp even if the last note is correct. Most players make this error because they are worried that the last slur, which is often the only difficult one, will not be correct. Another fault is in having no embouchure change for the last note, since the embouchure was already set for it too early. In other words, there is no embouchure change just where it is most needed—on the last slur. This problem is caused by nervousness at the difficulty of the slur and can be overcome by not allowing the final embouchure change to take place until the precise moment when it is needed. In the passage under discussion, for example, we must make absolutely certain that the next to last note is being played in tune. To do this we have to play the passage and stop on this note to listen to it before playing the last note. This is similar to the way of practicing a fingering problem. We must also train our ears to hear in a fast passage whether or not there are any notes out of tune.

Choice of Fingering

Some of the basic notes on the woodwind instruments can only be produced with one particular fingering. However, for many of the notes, there exist at least two, and, in many cases, quite a few different fingerings. Which fingering to choose depends on three factors: pitch, tone quality, and ease. Pitch, as we mentioned, depends on other factors besides the fingering, so that it is possible to have the correct pitch from a variety of fingerings. Of the other two factors, ease and tone quality, tone quality is most subject to personal taste. Here we find great differences in conception, especially from country to country. Although each person is quite sure of what he likes with regard to tone quality, it is not possible to give a scientific explanation of a "good tone." We must realize that the choice of fingering can greatly affect the tone quality. Actually the basic tone quality comes from such things as the instrument itself, the reed or mouthpiece, the embouchure, and so forth. What really concerns us here is to see that the various notes match each other as closely as possible. This is where the choice of fingerings becomes important. Two fingerings for the same note, producing the same pitch, can have extremely different tone qualities, almost as if they were played by two different players. We are discussing here the color of the sound. It would not be musically correct to play a scale in which the tone changed from note to note. Players, however, do learn to change the tone color for musical reasons. Therefore, while pitch is one of the crucial elements in deciding fingerings, we must give equal weight to tone quality. The most desirable set of fingerings would be those which would give good intonation and a matching of quality from note to note, with the greatest possible ease. This is extremely difficult and much compromising is necessary. Sometimes we have to sacrifice one or the other of the elements to solve a particular problem. For example, if a note sounds beautiful with a certain fingering, but is too difficult to play in tune, then we must sacrifice this fingering for one which will satisfy better the demands of both pitch and tone quality.

Together with tone quality the fingering can also affect dynamics. Some fingerings are simply louder than others. Here again we must find the fingerings that match the dynamics so that we do not have to compensate too much with the air. One of the dangers of a fingering chart is that it offers too many possibilities, and a beginner, who does not yet have sufficient control, could choose a completely unmatched set of fingerings without realizing it.

In the normal course of playing, all wind players learn which notes are likely to be out of tune on their instruments. They learn to compensate or to find corrective fingerings. This usually works well until they must play fast, difficult passages. Then a player could find that the fingering he chose is too difficult to use, or that there is no time for the compensation to be introduced. He must be flexible enough to drop his special fingering for an easier one. Even many of the normal fingerings are too difficult in very fast passages. In this case, special fingerings must be found. We introduce these fingerings only if the passage cannot otherwise be executed, and if the ear cannot detect the change; although in special cases, even though the ear can hear the alteration, it is the lesser of two evils. Fortunately the notes are often too fast for the ear to hear that either the pitch or the tone quality has been sacrificed. Too many players resort to these "false" fingerings, however, as a way of escaping the work necessary to make the right fingering possible. These players will often use a "false" fingering that can definitely be heard, simply because their standards are too low. We will resort to "false" fingerings only when other solutions do not work. Of course, if the passage is so difficult that there is only an even chance of its coming out with the right fingering, then we will probably use the "false" one.

With trills, the situation is different. Some trills work quite easily with the regular fingerings, while many others are completely impossible, and must find special trill fingerings. Here it is necessary to mention an important fact about "fake," or "false," fingerings. More often than not, they will only work if they are executed fast, rather than slow. That is, they only work properly during the actual playing of the passage or trill. There are two reasons for this. One is the inherent instability of some of the fingerings. They will produce the note, but will be unable to sustain it. The note "cracks" very quickly, but not too quickly to be used in a fast passage. This tells us that we cannot search for these fingerings by playing the notes slowly, because often they simply will not come out. The other reason is related to pitch. It is not possible to play both notes of a trill in tune, for example, because the embouchure cannot be altered back and forth at the speed of a trill. What we therefore do is to play instinctively the lower note in tune and let the upper one take care of itself. This usually works well in practice because the lower note is the key note. Therefore when we search for trill fingerings, we must not try to play the upper false fingered note by itself and expect it to be in tune. These fingerings should always be tried at the speed of the trill, then we must be sure to listen to determine if it sounds in tune. Of course there are some especially difficult trills that have both the fingerings altered, but here also we must listen to it at speed. Sometimes, in difficult passage work, it is found that the trill fingering is the best one to use. In choices of this kind, as in most other choices of technique, we must let our ear guide us. The ability to hear pitch and tone quality must be developed to as high a degree as possible during the playing of fast passages.

CHAPTER 5

BREATHING

Normal breathing is a natural act that is performed automatically. We can think about it if we wish, but when we do we find that it is almost impossible to imitate the easy flow of normal breathing. Playing a wind instrument is not, in this sense, a natural act and we must carefully learn how to breathe for it.

In our everyday activities, the amount of air taken in with each breath is quite small and would not allow for even the softest note on a wind instrument. We breathe deeply only when it is required, for instance as a consequence of strenuous exercise, and this type of breathing is also an automatic process. The body requires large amounts of air for such activity and it automatically puts certain muscles to work to obtain it as quickly as possible. Even greater quantities of air are required for coughing, sneezing, and yawning, acts which are also usually done without conscious thought. The wind player needs air not only for breathing but for operating his instrument as well. These separate needs usually go hand in hand, but sometimes they contradict each other, as we will soon see.

The amount of air able to be taken in varies a great deal from person to person; however, there is enough potentially available in even the smallest person to be able to play a wind instrument. This implies, of course, that this potential must be developed. The biggest problem is that people are not used to taking really deep breaths. Breathing deeply, unlike normal breathing, requires quite a bit of energy. It involves a number of muscles and the willingness to allow the lungs to fill so that the entire stomach area, chest, and back are extended to their limits. Breathing in this way will eventually greatly increase one's capacity. There are many phrases in music that use the absolute limits of one's breath capabilities. Besides the length of phrases, the amount of air determines how loudly a person can play.

The Physiology of Breathing

In order to take in large quantities of air, it is necessary to use as much of the lungs as possible; that is, they must not be restricted in any way. The lungs are capable of expanding much more than our ribs will allow them to. Thus the lungs do not set the limits, the stomach area and the rib cage do. When we breathe, we must allow these to be expanded by the lungs, but at the same time, we must aid this process. If we simply rely on the expanding lungs to do the work, we will severely limit our capacity because the lungs alone cannot handle so much work. We have to expand our ribs to the same degree that the lungs are expanding. The expanding of the ribs keeps pace with the lungs and therefore does not force them to do extra work. However, it is important that the ribs do not get too

87

far ahead of the lungs; they must work at exactly the same rate of speed. It is possible to expand the ribs and take in no air; this is also true of the stomach area. It is not the expansion of these muscles alone that is responsible for taking in air, but they can make it much easier and, in so doing, allow much more air to be taken in.

In addition to the problem of taking in large quantities of air, it is often necessary to take it in as quickly as possible. Whether or not we have to take a quick breath depends entirely on the music, but there is no doubt that it is often necessary and we must learn how to breathe quickly. Although this ability is not an everyday activity, it, too, comes with practice and the development of the muscles. It requires even more energy than deep breathing does because it must take place in a much shorter time.

In playing music, breathing should be tailored to each phrase played. It is not necessary always to take as large a breath as possible. When we take a deep breath, the natural tendency is to expel it fairly quickly. To hold back a deep breath requires a good deal of effort. This is the effort necessary to hold the ribs in their expanded state, but it is not necessary if the phrase to be played is a short one. There are phrases of all conceivable lengths, and there is an ideal amount of air for each one. This is the amount that will always leave a comfortable reserve after the phrase is finished. Emptying the lungs completely should always be avoided, but this is not always possible because some phrases are very long. When we do empty the lungs—besides the discomfort and lack of oxygen—it takes much longer to fill them than if there were a reserve. But, on the other hand, to play a short phrase with the lungs completely full is a great waste of energy and takes much more control just to hold back the air. It is most comfortable to play when the lungs are about one-third to two-thirds full, Since most phrases are only moderately long, this is a good compromise, and leaves ample reserves for an emergency. Of course, this presupposes a knowledge of the music being played or the ability to look ahead while sight reading in order to gauge the amount of air needed. If we are to make a mistake on how much air to take in, it should always be too much rather than too little.

Except in a very few special cases, we should breathe with the mouth rather than with the nose, because the opening from the mouth to the throat is much bigger than the opening from the nose to the throat. Hence, by using the same amount of energy, much more air can be taken into the lungs through the mouth than through the nose. We observe this in operation when we sneeze: the mouth opens wide so that as much air as possible can enter. The intake of air for a sneeze occurs rather slowly because we usually have a few seconds of warning. However, with a cough, the intake is as rapid as possible and is comparable to quick breathing. A great deal of energy is used when breathing through the mouth and the breath enters so rapidly that we can actually hear the rush of air. Too many players avoid making this kind of noise. Perhaps they feel that it is impolite, but if politeness is our main goal, then music is the wrong choice of profession.

In playing phrases which have difficult breathing problems, the player has two objectives: to take in as much air as possible and as quickly as possible. During fast breaths, there is rarely time to fill the lungs, so that we must depend on the speed of the intake to deliver as much air as possible. In many respects, a number of short breaths are often better than one long one. This is especially true when the phrases are connected rather than just single. If the player has a reasonable amount of rest at the end of a long phrase, then if possible he should do

89

it in one breath. However, if there is no rest, the player will be exhausted at the end of the phrase and out of breath; although the lungs are empty, he must continue, and a long breath is definitely needed. This situation always works to the detriment of the music. Four or five short breaths would have kept enough air in the player's lungs so that the next big breath could start with the lungs already partly filled. Often the music will allow for several short breaths where it wouldn't allow for one long one. A number of short breaths can also add up to one long, and very often it is helpful to take these short ones even when not needed so that we are ready for the long phrase soon to come. Figure 68 is an example of the type of writing that allows for short breaths in preparation for longer phrases.

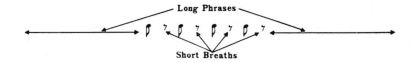

Figure 68.

Making Time to Breathe

Besides the use of the muscles to take in air, there is another important aspect of fast breathing: the exact instant that we start the breath. It is easy to see that a difference of only a fraction of a second can make a great difference in the amount of air taken in. This is related to the way in which the note before the breath is ended. Obviously, the sooner the note is ended, the more air can be taken in because of the extra time. Figure 69 shows four ways of ending the last note before the breath:

1. This is the way to get the most breath, but it sounds worst from a musical standpoint. It is used only as a last resort.
2. This ending is the one that sounds best, but leaves no time to breathe.
3. This is almost as good as (2), yet leaves some time to breathe. The amount of time to breathe may or may not be enough.
4. This best for quick breath. It sounds like (2) because the cutoff occurs at the soft part of the note, where it is less likely to be heard.

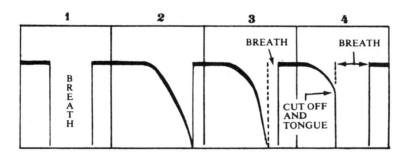

Figure 69.

Cutoff (3) is changed to cutoff (4) as follows: the instant that the cutoff occurs, the tongue is placed on the reed and, at that same instant, the breath is taken. Because of the taper on the note, the ear has the impression that the note goes on longer than it actually does. It takes a great deal of practice to end the note in this manner and to be prepared for the precise instant for the breath. We will recognize these diagrams from our discussion of resonant endings although here the cutoff is done purposely. Cutoff (4) might not sound well as the last note in a phrase because we might be able to hear the actual cutoff. However, in the middle of a phrase, between closely spaced notes, most likely it would not be noticed. It would either sound like a complete resonant ending, or the breath will not be noticed at all.

Another factor in quick breathing concerns the position of the embouchure during the breath. If we have plenty of time to breathe, or if there is a pause before the next phrase, we usually take the reed out of the mouth to rest the embouchure. Obviously there is not time for this in the kind of breathing under discussion. The less the embouchure is disturbed the better, because any altering must be corrected before the playing continues, and this takes time. The lips should be left as much in contact with the reed as possible and the embouchure altered as little as possible. This usually means that we breathe from the corners of the mouth, leaving the center pretty much in its original position. Of course, the more time we have, the farther the embouchure is removed from the reed. Many people forget that it is only the lower jaw that is able to move; the upper one always remaining fixed unless we raise the entire head. It is therefore much easier and quicker to breathe by lowering the bottom jaw than by raising the upper one. This applies particularly to the bassoon.

Judging the Amount of Air Needed

It is not always possible to judge correctly the amount of air needed for a particular phrase. If we have taken too little, then the problem becomes a musical one in which the player must find a spot to breathe that will least disturb the phrase. It is often possible to make the breath become a musical part of the phrase, even when it was not specifically intended by the composer. Many phrases have points in them that are resting places, or places that have little energy. These may possibly lend themselves to a breath. They will be discussed further in a later chapter.

The other type of misjudgment is taking in too much breath. Here the problem is twofold: first, there is the discomfort connected with having too much air, and second, there is the problem of having to expel the extra air before being able to take another breath. This takes time. A player with some experience knows very soon after the phrase has been started whether or not he has too much breath. He can then expel some of the air through the corners of his mouth while he is playing. With practice this can be done with almost no disturbance of the embouchure. The oboist in particular has the problem of too much air. Very often after a long phrase we will notice that the oboist will expel air while the others will take it in. This is because of the very small opening through which the player blows. He plays with greater pressure, but uses less air.

There are now a few players, particularly oboists, who use a new technique for unlimited breath, called circular breathing. This is really not new at all, but it is new as applied to Western music. Besides being used in Eastern music, this technique is in widespread use by glassblowers, who must keep up a steady stream of air for much longer than a single breath would allow. The idea is to be able to breathe in through the nose at the same time that one is blowing through the mouth. This is accomplished by filling the mouth and cheeks with air and using the cheeks to force the air through the reed while breathing in through the nose. The difficulties concern the transition between one type of blowing and the other. It is very difficult to make this transition smoothly so that we do not hear a change in pitch. This technique may only be applied to the oboe because the other winds usually require

much more air than the cheeks can hold. It is a little iron-
ic that the oboe can perform this technique, because this
instrument has less difficulty with long phrases than any
of the other winds.

Exercises

In order to make certain that we are taking in
enough air, it is necessary to overdo it consciously for a
while. Take extremely long breaths before long notes and
long phrases.

For quick breathing and for the ability to take a number of short breaths instead of one long one, we should
perform regular exercises but put in many extra breaths:
1. Watch for the proper ending to the note before the
    breath. Breathing should not destroy musical consi-
    derations.
2. Gradually try to shorten the time necessary for the
    breath.
3. Gradually increase the amount of air taken in during
    quick breaths.

PART II

MUSICIANSHIP

CHAPTER *6*

STYLE

So far, we have been dealing with mechanical techniques. Now we will examine how to apply them to music. No technique is an end in itself, but rather the means to the end of expressing oneself. Although the playing of music is in itself composed of many mechanical operations, our goal is anything but mechanical. It is very much like the process of learning to speak a language, during which there are many mechanical operations to perform and endless practice. During this long practice period, we must make use of all mechanical operations, but for a long time we make very little sense and are not able to do anything "naturally." All the mechanical operations are aimed at eventually enabling us to express ideas and feelings which have nothing to do with mechanical operations. The mechanics can be methodically taught, but the expression must ultimately come from the individual. This section of the book is an attempt to explain how all these diverse mechanical operations are put together to allow us to play in a musical way. The author is not trying to show the correct way to play, because he does not believe in such a concept as "the one right way." Rather he will show the manner in which the various techniques might be applied and the results of altering them. The techniques must serve the purpose of expressing what each individual desires to express, but such expression is impossible without technique.

The Evolution of Style

Music has a long history during which it has changed greatly. It has passed through many different styles and will continue to do so. These changes are more or less gradual, and it is often difficult to find any boundaries between the various styles. When we speak of style, we mean everything that composes a particular period of history.

Style is perhaps easier to understand as applied to something tangible like clothes. Clothing styles are continually changing, and moreover these styles fall into a number of larger categories. We are sure of the differences because we can see them in paintings or photographs or museum exhibits. The case with music, however, is quite different. It is only in this century that recordings have enabled us to hear how music was performed. For the styles prior to this century, we must rely on tradition, which at best is vague and capricious. So-called tradition has led to many distortions and inaccuracies. Of course, we can always turn to the music itself. But the problem here is that it is a truism that a composer cannot put down on paper more than about thirty percent of what he actually has in his mind. The actual percentage is not important; what is important is that we realize that most of his intentions cannot be put down. The realization of those inten-

97

tions is left to the performer and to the performer's under-standing of the composer's use of the musical language. A large part of this understanding has to do with style.

There are many extraneous elements that influence the making of a style of a particular art-form. These in-fluences reflect the life of the times and include, among others, political, moral, and social issues. However, what will concern us here is simply those issues that have to do with the actual performance of music, primarily the tech-niques and playing practices of the times.

Most great composers of the past were also practical musicians who were able to perform the works they wrote. Some of them were among the outstanding instrumental-ists of their day. They never wrote works that were impos-sible to perform, although some were very difficult. These composers were obviously under the influence of the play-ing practices of their day, and completely conversant with them. The composer's vision would always find ways to display the performer's abilities. Often, the performers themselves developed new ways of playing and therefore influenced the composers. Instrument makers were also responsible for some of the gains in the technical excel-lence of players. And the actual performing conditions of the day also had an influence on style. In our discussion the following styles will be considered: Renaissance, Ba-roque, Classical, Romantic, and Modern.

RENAISSANCE

One of the main characteristics of the music of the Renaissance (which is extremely relevant for our pur-poses) was an almost total lack of flexibility of dynamics. This was a direct result of the way in which the instru-ments were constructed. There were a large number of different instruments, divided into families. Each family had a soprano, alto, tenor, and bass whose only difference was in the size of the instrument. This was necessary because each instrument had a very narrow range, and, in order to cover the range from high to low, all four members of the family were needed. Each family had its own characteristic timbre and dynamic. Some were called loud instruments, some soft. Almost none of our present day instruments existed at that time. Wind instruments were usually loud, and strings (that is lutes and viols), soft. The reason each family was limited to one basic dynamic was in the construction of the instruments. If we examine the lute, we will find that it has frets placed on the fingerboard to give the correct intonation and keep the string from being damped by the soft tip of the finger. This fact, and the fact that the strings were placed very close to the fingerboard and the raised frets, meant that the string would buzz if it were plucked too hard because in vibrating the string would hit the frets. Besides this, the shape of the body was not chosen in order to produce a loud sound but rather a mellow one.

A similar situation existed for the winds, especially the reed instruments. The lack of flexibility will become apparent when we examine the recorder, which was one of the most important families of wind instrument. The recorder has a fixed mouthpiece. This means that the player's lips can have no effect on the instrument. When we play the recorder it is only a matter of supplying the correct amount of air. If either more or less air is put into it, the note will be out of tune, and if even more is put in, the note will stop, or go up an octave. From this we know that the recorder has a limited dynamic range. During the Renaissance, in playing many of the reed instruments, the players had not conceived the idea of placing the lips on the reed. In many cases, the reed was placed inside the instrument, and the player could not touch it even if he wanted to. We know that each reed at a particular opening requires a critical amount of air to cause it to vibrate. Any deviation will cause the note to go out of tune, or to stop. Since the reeds were never touched by the lips, there was only one opening and therefore only one dynamic. Some of the instruments had the reed placed entirely inside the mouth, with the teeth touching the back of the reed, but not the lips. The bagpipe is one of the few remaining examples of a Renaissance-type instrument. In the bagpipe, the reed is placed inside the instrument and the player only has to blow through a pipe and supply enough air. None of these instruments required an embouchure as we know it. The reeds at that time were quite different from each other. Some were very heavy and meant to produce loud sounds, while others were very small and soft in order to produce a very gentle sound. The sounds themselves were very different because for one thing the reeds were vibrating in free air. By and large, they were also much heavier than the reeds of today.

It appears that vibrato was not in widespread use, if at all. Vibrato is also a very risky practice on fretted instruments because of the tendency to buzz. It is probable that instrumentalists gradually learned about vibrato from the voice, which was always capable of producing it, and it might have taken a hundred or more years to come into general use. Vibrato seems not to have been used on the strings until after the introduction of the violin family, which was well after the Renaissance.

The musical style of the Renaissance, therefore, consisted of a combination of the compositional devices in use by the composers, as applied to the capabilities inherent in the instruments themselves. Homogeneity of sound existed only between instruments of the same family, and dynamics became associated with particular sound qualities. When the composer wanted to shift the dynamics, he had to change to another family of instruments. The musical thinking of the day was very blocklike. Much of the music was performed in churches, which have very reverberant acoustical properties. These properties make all sounds much louder than they would be elsewhere. They also make it almost impossible to play short notes because the reverberation of the building is so great. It is not uncommon for the decay time in a church to be five or more seconds. Besides this, the bows of the string instruments would not allow the player to produce short notes, nor could most of the wind players cut the notes short without causing the pitch to change because of the lack of contact between the lips and the reed. Plucked instruments sounded best when the notes were allowed to ring. Counterpoint, the prevalent compositional device of the times, gave equal importance to all the lines, making individuality, as we know it, unnecessary.

To sum up the stylistic qualities of Renaissance, we have:

1. Families of instruments, playing within a very narrow dynamic range.
2. Crescendo and diminuendo not a part of the vocabulary.
3. Practically no use of short notes.
4. No vibrato.
5. Dynamics unspecified, since they were a function of whatever instrument was playing.
6. Little individual expression as we know it.
7. No subtleties of attack or ending of notes.

BAROQUE

Between the Renaissance and the Baroque periods, a great deal of experimentation took place toward the creation of new instruments. All kinds of things were tried, some truly outlandish. By the time of the Baroque, an al-

101

most completely different set of instruments existed. The idea of complete families had all but disappeared, except for the recorder family and the new family of stringed instruments. Instead of a family of oboes, or bassoons, there was the one dominant member of each family—along with the then newly popular flute—to make up the woodwind family. This family no longer had a homogeneity of sound; rather each member, while certainly recognizable as a wind instrument, had its own distinct sound.

Composers no longer wanted to be made to change from one instrument to another whenever they wanted a different dynamic. Their search for greater dynamic flexibility led to profound changes in the nature of the instruments. The fretted stringed instruments were giving way to the newly developed violin family. Their superiority was quickly recognized, and the fact that the instruments reached perfection made their dominance complete. Many instrument makers spent their lives in developing this perfection, and during the Cremona period, there were such master builders as Stradivarius, Guarnerius, Amati, and many others, whose instruments have not been surpassed to this day.

During the period from the Baroque to the Classical, there was one other revolutionary change taking place in the strings. This concerned the bow. Until that time, the main purpose of the bow was to sustain long tones. This bow was called the curved bow, its actual curve varying from time to time and from country to country.

There was relatively little tension in this bow as compared to the modern bow. Until then, there had not been a need for greater tension; music was played mostly "on the string," which consisted of moving the bow back and forth without lifting it. However, with the developing desire to play shorter notes and to play more loudly, the need for a different bow was becoming evident. The relative slackness of the curved bow made it difficult to have definite, incisive attacks, and this undoubtedly caused composers to avoid writing that kind of music, or even conceive it. But on the new bow, the hair was so taut that it could bounce with ease, and these bounces made possible shorter and shorter notes.

It is possible to create much greater tension in the modern bow because the hairs are tightened against a virtually straight piece of wood. The realization of the potential for short notes, and the development of a bow technique for it, took many years to achieve, lasting well into the Classical era.

While this revolution was taking place in the strings, similar revolution was taking place in the winds. Reed instruments, in which the player's lips did not touch the reed, were gradually supplanted, first by the shawn, then by the oboes and bassoons. The oboes and bassoons were played in the modern manner, and this gave them a control over dynamics and pitch which was previously impossible. Not only are the dynamics dependent on the use of the lips, but adjustments to the pitch as well.

At the beginning of the Baroque era recorders constituted one of the important wind families, but it became apparent that they had several serious limitations. First, their dynamic range was severely limited because of the fixed nature of the mouthpiece. Second, their tonal range was rather narrow. Also, as the oboe and the bassoon became louder, it became more difficult for the recorder to balance with them. The flute, called at that time transverse flute to distinguish it from the recorder, had been in existence for centuries. Indeed it is one of the oldest instruments of any kind. One of the reasons that had kept the flute out of the general musical life was that it did not have the four members in its family that other winds had. This rather restricted its role. However, as the instruments became restricted to one kind in each range, the flute became the obvious choice for the soprano role. (It is interesting to note that about a hundred years later the opposite was to happen; that is, there was a search for more instruments in each family to extend the range.) This process took many years to accomplish, and during the interim there was much music written for some of the transitional instruments, such as the oboe d'amore, and for brass instruments of many different sizes. But the main reason for the superiority of the flute over the recorder lies in the fact that the lips are part of the mouthpiece and can alter the size of the opening to correct intonation and to allow for loud and soft dynamics.

The harpsichord was the most important keyboard instrument of the Baroque era. It produces sound by a plucking action on the strings, and can only produce one dynamic at a time. The sound thus produced does not depend on how hard the key is struck, but rather on the fixed action of the plectrum on the string. There were many ingenious solutions developed to compensate for this limitation, such as multiple strings, two keyboards, and couplers that allowed two sets of strings to be played at once, but these innovations still resulted in only block changes in dynamics with no possibility for shadings or crescendo-diminuendo. Harpsichords grew considerably in size over the years. This was an attempt to keep up with the use of larger and larger ensembles. The limitations of the harpsichord led to the development of the piano, or as it was originally called, forte-piano or piano-forte. The name was an indication of its revolutionary qualities. Even on the early forte-pianos it was possible to play a fairly large range of dynamics. The piano was not introduced until after the start of the Classical period, but its development was an inevitable result of the search for greater dynamic flexibility.

One of the most important elements of style in the Baroque era was the use of ornamentation. Ornamentation consists in adding additional notes to the ones that have been specified by the composer. Its purpose is to heighten, intensify, or fill in what the composer has set down. In many cases the composer has himself indicated which ornament he desires, but in most cases the choice is left to the performer, and it was expected that the performer would do so. This practice left room for him to express his own ideas up to a point, and it is the author's belief that ornamentation was the main area of personal expression at that time. The freedom of choice in the use of ornamentation inevitably led to such extremes that it might become impossible to recognize the composer's original intentions. This occurred at the end of the Baroque and led Bach to write out his ornaments so that he could be sure of having his intentions realized. A similar situation was to exist in the Classical era in connection with the cadenza.

There are many different types of ornaments, ranging from the addition of a single note to florid scales and arpeggios. Anyone who plays Baroque music must acquaint himself with the many types of ornaments and their use if he is to remain faithful to the style. It is not the purpose of this book to discuss the use of ornaments. However, we must recognize their importance to the Baroque style as a means of largely personal expressiveness. This expressiveness was achieved by altering the pitches rather than by the way in which the written notes were played.

It is still a matter of dispute, whether or not vibrato was in use at this time, but in the author's opinion it played at best a very minor role. Its ability to act as an expressive device was hardly conceivable and only became possible as the modern Baroque instruments were developed.

Although dynamic flexibility was becoming more and more of a possibility, there was relatively little use of subtleties. Composers still rarely indicated dynamics and must have continued to be influenced by the blocklike dynamics of the Renaissance. The players still had to learn to use

105

the whole range of dynamics that was becoming available to them, and this involved a greater and greater understanding and use of the embouchure. Along with this there was a need for higher standards in the making of reeds and instruments. The use of shorter, or detached, notes was only cautiously employed because techniques for their production were being experimented with.

To sum up the Baroque in terms of instrumental characteristics, there were:

1. A moderate dynamic range, from p to f, still often in blocks.
2. The beginning of the use of crescendo, diminuendo, but sparingly.
3. Some use of shorter notes, but not a true staccato.
4. Relatively little use of vibrato.
5. A great deal of attention to ornamentation.
6. Relatively little use of color and dynamic changes on individual notes.

CLASSICAL

The Classical period emerged because of a desire, on the one hand, to do away with excesses in the use of ornamentation and, on the other, because a point of saturation had been reached in the contrapuntal style. This period saw the development of single-line writing, and the melody as such became much more important. Ornamentation, except for the simplest kinds such as trills, turns, and mordents, had ceased to be used. The composers preferred to have their lines played as they had conceived them, which meant that they had to be as complete and as perfect as possible. The idea of interpretation had to take a different direction from that of altering the notes on the printed page. Architectural perfection and balance were a goal of the Classical period, and the search for these led to the development of the sonata allegro form. The many forms that existed at that time were distilled to a relatively few archetypal models such as sonata allegro, song form, minuet and trio, rondo, and variations. These became the superstructure upon which the beautifully balanced melodies could be placed. In sonata allegro, the opening phrase, together with the answering phrase, could become the basis for an entire movement, and therefore had to be as perfect and as complete as possible. This perfection was one of balance, almost of the shape of the line. Composers had to search for laws that governed the new possibilities in music; they were certainly not self-evident. They would not emerge in their entirety until geniuses like Haydn and Mozart created them.

The instruments continued to develop along the lines that were started in the Baroque era. The strings were learning to exploit the potentialities inherent in the newly developed bow. The winds depended more and more upon the embouchure, and the instruments themselves were gradually improved. This led to a larger range of dynamics and compass of notes. The clarinet was introduced and became a member of the newly developing orchestra. Trumpets were also added as regular members. The size of orchestras also grew over the years. Increasingly, use was made of the crescendo and the diminuendo, although the overall range was still relatively small. Only one or two of each woodwind was used and these were able to balance the small string section of that day. The brasses were rather subdued to balance with the other instruments. Short notes were used more often and the concept of "staccato" was developed along with the new symbol for it—the dot. This was partly due to the new bow which could so easily bounce on the strings. Vibrato continued to develop, but still at a slow pace, and we begin to find reference to it in method books.

To sum up the Classical period, we find:

1. A dynamic range from p to f, with pp and ff seldom used at first.
2. Violent contrasts sparingly used.
3. More emphasis on beauty of tone.
4. Vibrato more in use, but sparingly.
5. Staccato introduced.
6. Careful, clean execution became a goal.
7. Vocabulary of string bowing technique enlarged.
8. Composers beginning to give more directions as to their intent.
9. Expressiveness a function of beauty and balance rather than of color or vibrato.

ROMANTIC

Both the end of the Classical period and the beginning of the Romantic period were dominated by Beethoven; he brought one to an end and helped create the other. By contrast, Bach summed up an entire era and brought it to its highest peak of perfection, but did not go beyond it. Beethoven shattered the completeness and balance of the Classical period and plunged ahead into the turmoil and emotionality of the Romantic. At the time, it seemed as though Beethoven were breaking all the established rules, while in reality he was actually creating new ones. Most composers are content to live within the rules, even when those rules have outlived their usefulness. But any conception, however great, must sooner or later become stale and become a hindrance to further progress. No matter how perfectly a given "truth" fits a particular set of circumstances, inevitably those circumstances will change. When that happens, a new "truth" is found only through the destruction of the old.

Any artist's work must express the time in which he lives and Beethoven's time was a passionate one, full of violence and revolution. Gradually, through his life, we find the older ideas of purity and balance of architectural forms replaced by violent contrasts and sudden changes of direction. These were expressions of impetuousness and individuality that continued throughout his life, and were taken up by others after him.

The orchestra continued to grow, although when Beethoven's First Symphony was given its première, it employed only thirty-three players. This is in marked contrast to the situation when his Ninth Symphony was played. Not only was the orchestra very much larger, but the work also had four solo voices and a large chorus. Symphonies had grown in length as well as in size. The early symphonies of Haydn were usually less than twenty minutes long, while Mozart's last symphony was less than thirty minutes in length, but the Ninth Symphony of Beethoven lasts for over an hour. The orchestra had already enlarged to two of each wind so as to allow the winds and growing string section to balance. Later in the Romantic era two more horns were added, and soon the trombones became regular members, followed by the tuba. By this time, the woodwinds were doubled so that there were up to four each, with at least one player doubling on piccolo, English horn, E♭ and bass clarinets, and contrabassoon. Four timpani were commonly used, and a number of other percussion players were required. The harp was added and the string section became almost as large as the one in use today.

All these changes allowed the composer great latitude in his choice of dynamics and tone color. Fortissimos, three, four, or five *f*'s, were used along with the correspondingly soft markings, down to five, or six *p*'s. We find great use made of the *sfz*, and even this was enlarged to the *sffz*. New tone colors were discovered and used. In the strings, special effects such as *ponticello, col legno,* and the growing use of harmonics, were developed. The brass instruments were able to change their tone a great deal by using different mutes, and the French horn players could produce a unique sound by stopping the horn completely with the hand to produce a "brassy" sound, called *quivre*. In the percussion section many instruments were added for special effects, including chimes, which were used to simulate church bells, gongs, cymbals, and even a wind machine.

Vibrato became a powerful tool in expressing the passionate feelings and changes of mood of that period. It was fully developed in the strings and was gradually becoming so in the winds. Oboes, flutes, and bassoons developed it first. It had become so flexible that it could be used on only a single note, or it could be started and stopped in the middle of a note or phrase. It also had a greater range of speed and amplitude, which could also be altered at will. The use of expressive devices, such as vibrato and changing tone color, were to become the most important way of shaping a line.

To sum up the Romantic era, we have:

1. A dynamic range from as soft as possible to as loud as possible.
2. Sudden dramatic changes of dynamic, even for one note.
3. Very many new directions from composers, such as: *calando, sffz, con brio,* and so forth.
4. Emotional, sensual playing; expression of utmost importance.
5. Great use of vibrato, with much flexibility.
6. Regular use of staccato.

CONTEMPORARY

Each period in music history contains its own truths and laws. They are certainly not apparent at the beginning of an era, and are only gradually uncovered. It is the insight of the great composers that points the way. It seems that new laws do not appear until the old ones have been thoroughly tested and explored so that there is nothing left to be learned from them. Such was the case at the end of the Romantic era. The reaction against it took several different forms. Some tried consciously to mix styles from the past with modern concepts of harmony and orchestration. These resulted in what was called Neo-Baroque or Neo-Classical. Stravinsky was at various times involved in these forms. A more revolutionary approach was taken by Schoenberg, who developed the twelve-tone system in an effort to make a complete break with the past. Before that time, Schoenberg was a perfect example of a composer of Romantic music. One of the main characteristics of Romantic music was the use of chromatic harmony. The harmonic vocabulary was constantly expanding throughout the Romantic era to the point where all the older rules of harmonic progression were stretched to the breaking point. It was in this area that Schoenberg decided to break with the past in establishing the twelve-tone system. In this system, all the notes of the chromatic scale were given equal importance, and chords as we knew them ceased to exist. A piece was written around a "row" which contained all twelve tones arranged in a particular order. The ordering of the notes in the row was the important factor. The row was meant to be altered in as many as forty-eight ways, and mathematical manipulation became an important element. This brief description of twelve-tone music is highly oversimplified since it is beyond the purpose of this book to analyze any particular system of music. A number of books explaining this system are available. Our concern here is with style, and while Schoenberg pointed the way toward a radically new method of composition, his style remained very much in the Romantic tradition. It remained for his disciples, notably Webern, to develop a completely new style based on the potentialities inherent in Schoenberg's ideas.

Webern ultimately separated all the parameters of music and treated them as independent elements. He did not carry these ideas to their conclusion, but definitely brought them out into the open. The development of his ideas has continued throughout this century and still continues. It has led to the complete serialization of music in one school of modern composition. In this school, the various elements of music, such as pitch, rhythm, dynamics, register, duration, and mode of attack can all be subjected to mathemathical manipulation. This manipulation can be arrived at through the use of computers, to mention just one of the possibilities. Other schools of composition depend on improvisation or aleatoric principles having to do with chance or randomness. Many of the ideas concerning chance music have come from the American composer John Cage and his followers.

Twelve-tone, or serial, music is very difficult to perform because the notes in the composition relate to each other in totally different ways from those in the music of the past. The idea of a line, or melody, in which the notes relate to each other to express the shape, harmony, or balance of the phrase, is no longer applicable. Instead, each note is an entity that contains several distinct elements. These could include the type of attack, which would have nothing to do with the rest of the note, its dynamic, and its duration. Each of these elements fulfills its own function in the mathematical scheme of the composition. The performer, therefore, needs much more precise control than was formerly necessary. The blending and leading of one note into another is now inappropriate unless that particular set of parameters should be called for, which is

rather unlikely since most contemporary composers try to

avoid those qualities that are reminiscent of the music of the past.

Another area of difficulty concerns range, both of pitch and dynamics. Since the Baroque era, the ranges of the instruments have been continually expanding, particularly the woodwinds. Sometimes the instrument makers were responsible for the expanding range, but more often the performers themselves found new fingerings and new ways of using the embouchure in order to play increasingly higher. This process is still going on. The oboe, for example, is now expected to play higher than the flute did just two generations ago, and the flute is up at least a fourth higher than it was a few generations ago. At that time, it could only play high C at an *ff* dynamic and with a very rough, noisy sound. Now it is expected to play this note at any dynamic and with a beautiful tone. The woodwinds are now asked to play with different timbres and to play harmonics which require special fingerings. Tremolos, which were thought to be impossible, are often used, as are glissandos and intervals of less than half a step.

There are a number of other new techniques being developed, some by players and some by composers. One of the newest of these is the playing of multiple notes at the same time to produce double, triple, or even quadruple stops. This technique is also used to give musical sounds with certain types of noise components. There are two methods for the production of these combination tones. One involves new fingerings and the other involves completely different settings of the air-embouchure combination. Much of the basic research in this field has been done by the Italian composer Bruno Bartolozzi. Until today, fingerings have been pretty well standardized, and it only remained to find the proper setting of the air-embouchure combination to produce the desired note. In order to play combination tones, we must consider the *113* three elements, air, embouchure, and fingering, as independent of each other. Then it is necessary to find the correct settings for each of these which will produce the desired results. In traditional terms, it is necessary to play the wrong settings to produce combination tones. Generally, the embouchure setting is much looser than would be expected. For example, we play a type of fingering that is characteristic of the higher notes, while using an embouchure that is appropriate for a rather low note.

It is clear that to execute some of the newer techniques we must do things that we have been specifically taught to avoid. It is still too early to tell, but if this technique of combination tones should become an accepted one, then it will be necessary for players to learn several sets of fingerings and air-embouchure settings. Not all the new techniques that are tried will become established as a part of the general playing repertoire, but some of them are bound to. For example, the strings have over the years had to learn to deal with the mute, harmonics, *col legno,* snap pizzicato, and recently playing behind the bridge and on the tail piece. These things are all part of the composer's search for new sounds, a search that has always taken place and presumably will continue to do so.

One of the relatively new techniques for the winds is the use of flutter-tonguing. It was first employed in the early part of this century by such different composers as Richard Strauss and Schoenberg. Strauss used it to imitate the sounds made by sheep, while Schoenberg and many composers after him considered it simply another quality of sound. It is interesting to note that even today there are still a great many players who do not know how to produce it. This may be done in either of two ways; with the front or with the back of the tongue. The flute and the brass use the front of the tongue, while the oboe, bassoon, and clarinet use the back of the tongue. The flute and the brass could use the back of the tongue, but they obtain better results with the front; the clarinet can use the front, although with some difficulty. The front or tip of the tongue is placed against the back of the upper teeth and held there with a moderate amount of pressure so that when the air stream passes around it on its way into the instrument the tongue at a certain point will start to vibrate or flutter. This will cause the air going into the instrument to start and stop many times per second to produce the fluttering sound that is the main characteristic of this technique. It is harder to produce this sound with the back of the tongue against the throat, but it is certainly possible. The oboe, clarinet, and bassoon must use this method because the reed protrudes well into the mouth, making it impossible to use the tip of the tongue. The sound produced with the back of the tongue is not as extreme as that produced with the tip, but is nevertheless acceptable. It may help to think of the sound of the front being the letter *r* as it is used in Spanish and Italian and of the back being the *r* as it is used in French. The back *r* is also the sound produced by gargling with a liquid.

Other new techniques involve bringing the fingers down hard on the keys, either with or without playing the note, to produce a pitched key click. This is especially effective on the flute, but has been used on all the winds. There is also a new technique which involves humming a particular note while playing either the same note or another. This will produce either the two notes, or a gurgling noise, or even three different notes. A very interesting technique is to hum, using a glissando, which causes a changing series of effects. There are other, more or less interesting "tricks" which are being explored, but many of them are only the product of one particular composer and have not been taken into the general repertoire of techniques. However, some of them are bound to come into

115

widespread use and then it will be necessary for wind players to learn them.

The use of wide skips from note to note was introduced in the Romantic era and is now considered a normal part of playing. The continuous use of large skips is not considered a new technique but rather an extension of the traditional way of playing. That is, no new techniques are required, but simply the refining of an ability that already exists. This is to a certain extent also true of the newer way in which vibrato is being used. Here the composer will often specify how the vibrato is to be done. It may start slowly and make an accelerando, or it may become much wider than normal, or it may employ any of the other variations that are possible in connection with the speed and amplitude of the vibrato.

In summing up Contemporary music, we have:
1. Extremes of range, especially on the high end.
2. Full range of dynamics for any note.
3. Great attention to the precise notation: dynamics, duration, type of attack, and so forth.
4. Separation of the various elements of a sound into their component parts.
5. Ability to make the largest possible skips.
6. Many special effects.
7. Vibrato, often specified by the composer as to speed or amplitude.
8. Less "emotional" playing. Playing more in terms of isolated, pure sound events.
9. Great emphasis on sound as an end in itself.

In terms of performers, style and performing practice are synonymous, and performing practice has differed greatly from period to period. Of course it is not always possible to draw precise lines, and much overlapping occurs from one style to another. Too many performers are limited, however, to only one style of performance. Many of them are simply not aware of the differences that exist between styles and would play music of the Baroque, Romantic, and Modern periods in the same—usually Romantic—manner. Other performers, who realize that their way of playing is not compatible with certain periods, will avoid those periods and will "specialize" in only one period. This type of performer is perhaps best exemplified by some of our famous soloists, and since there exists so much solo and concerto music from the Romantic period, it is easy to see why they have become exponents of Romantic music.

Most musicians, however, will not be among the small handful of famous soloists who can exist only by performing the music of one style. To many listeners there is nothing more abhorrent than to hear a Baroque piece played in the Romantic manner or a Romantic piece played in the Baroque style. People will always be fascinated, awed, and delighted by displays of dazzling technique, but we must realize that music has many other things to express and in order to be able to express them an understanding and appreciation of style are first necessary.

CHAPTER 7

INTERPRETATION

We do not reproduce music; we interpret it. If it were simply a matter of reproducing it, there would only be one way to play each piece and the world of music would be incredibly dull. Fortunately we are not faced with this situation (except in the area of electronic music) because no two people play alike, and, what is more important, the composer is at best only able to put down on paper about thirty percent of his intentions. The rest is left to the interpretation of the performer. Interpretation is the sum total of a person's technical abilities and his musical understanding. Musical understanding includes rhythm, harmony, and style, while technique embraces such things as finger technique, intonation, and tone, and so forth. All these are brought into play at the actual performance itself. The performer becomes the means of bringing the work of art to life, and in the process of interpretation he must inevitably contribute something of himself. For a good musician, a contribution of thirty percent from the composer is enough because they speak the same language; for a poor musician, thirty percent is hopelessly inadequate.

In discussing the variables in interpreting a composer's intentions we find that there is only one which is not subject to the kind of interpreting under discussion, and that is pitch. (At the moment we are not discussing some of the newest aleatoric music in which the choice of note might be left to the performer.) It is possible, however, to alter the pitch somewhat at the start of a note, especially on the strings, by sliding the fingers, but the object is still to produce the notated pitch. The other parameters of music, which remain extremely variable, are time (rhythm) and volume (dynamics), with vibrato in a separate category.

In this book we will not attempt the study of harmony. However, an understanding of harmony, whether intellectual or instinctual, is absolutely necessary to a complete understanding of music. Much of the music of this century, and almost all of the music of the past, rests upon the foundation of harmonic progression. This is true whether or not we are speaking of a single line or of many lines. In interpreting a piece, our understanding of harmonic progression plays one of the most important roles. The importance of any single note is a result of its function in the harmonic scheme of the work. Just how much importance and how it is expressed is a matter for one's own interpretation. One definition of interpretation might be that it is the manner in which notes are emphasized in relation to their comparative importance. There are a number of these which can be used, and they will now be explained. We will not attempt to say which is right and which is wrong; such a concept as right and wrong is far too limiting, since so many degrees of both exist. Rather it will be for the student to apply them as he sees fit or as his taste dictates. At the same time, we must remember that before something can be used in an organic way, it must be thoroughly learned, but that during the learning process it will remain more or less artificial.

Time and Speed

We accept and use the term "perfect pitch" as meaning that it is possible to remember the precise pitches used in music. Even though recent studies have shown that a person's pitch perception can be altered according to his emotional state, we still think of perfect pitch in terms of an absolute. But no one ever says "perfect time" or "perfect rhythm," for we realize that in the area of time things are relative.

Most composers have very definite ideas about exactly at what speed their music should be played. But their ideas vary from time to time and many of them change their minds as soon as they have heard the piece played. Since the end of the Classical period, the metronomic indication has been placed at the beginning of a piece to show how fast it is to be played, for example ♩ = 112. We can find this speed by setting the metronome. However, this speed can, in practice, only be relatively correct; it is not possible, or even desirable, to remain at one speed. There is, however, a small group of contemporary composers to whom the precise duration of notes is one of the most important parameters. Yet even for these composers the relationship of the duration of notes is more important than the actual speed of the piece, since a performer cannot maintain a precise speed for more than a short time. In any case, aside from the metronome, the idea of "fast" and "slow" has changed in the course of music history. This could be partly because of the ever faster pace of life or because performers are always improving on the techniques of the past and are often able to play faster now than in previous times. We are therefore faced with the fact that speed or tempo is not a fixed, unalterable quantity. The metronome can only be a guide and will at best produce an average overall speed for a given work, a speed that will vary in response to the living flow of the music. Music of the past sounds dull and mechanical when it is played in a rigid, metronomic way. Life, after all, is anything but rigidly predictable, and art has always been a reflection of life. We will see shortly how the varying of speed is used consciously as a means of expression, and that it is one of the most powerful tools for that purpose.

Time Signature—An Architectural Conception

Throughout most of the history of music, the downbeat, and its inevitable partner the bar line, has been one of the most fundamental building units of musical composition. Bar lines, which delineate the measures, occur regularly throughout the entire piece, and each measure has its own downbeat. The downbeat has a different sound from the other beats in the measure, usually because of an extra degree of stress. Harmonic progression also follows the rules regarding the downbeat stress. In other words, the downbeat usually contains the most important and meaningful musical statement of the measure. Of course, composers often deviate from this pattern, but they do so in the full knowledge that they are deviating from a norm. Music does not simply consist of a long series of equally stressed beats, because if there were not frequent deviations, the result would be a total lack of shape, growth, or change. Beyond the stressing of the downbeat, there exists in the measure a hierarchy of relative importance for *121* the other beats. Moreover, this architectural conception of the varying degrees of importance changes as the time signature changes.

We must realize that at the moment we are speaking only in an average and general way, and that these innate structures are constantly being modified and even contradicted by the composer in a purposeful way from an accepted foundation. It is also misleading to consider a single measure out of the context of the larger phrase, in which the smaller architectural shape would be subordinated to the larger shape of the overall phrase. Yet even here the rules of downbeat stress are applied, except that, for example, one downbeat could easily be much louder than another, with the result that the weaker notes in one measure could also be louder than the downbeat of another measure. The overall shape of the phrase is more important than any individual measure.

It can be said, therefore, that each measure has its own life, but that this individuality is meant to be dependent on the life of the larger unit, the phrase.

The architecture of a measure is influenced by the speed of the piece as well as the particular time signature. As music becomes faster it becomes more and more difficult to introduce subtleties of stress, and at a certain speed there will only be time to make the downbeat stresses. Nevertheless, it is part of the really good musician's technique to be able to emphasize notes even at fast speeds.

The term "stress" has been employed to describe a fairly complex set of variables, but basically these variables concern time and volume, with vibrato able to interact with either. The amount and type of stress used is of the utmost importance to their musical success. It is just such decisions that constitute "interpretation." This is especially true since there is no "scientific" way that can be of any use to the player; he must make the decisions. A

122

composer is unable to write down all the nuances that he might conceive; a language contains within it much more than the cold facts would seem to indicate, provided it is really understood.

The amount and type of stress applied is in a sense up to the performer. These decisions are partly a result of the player's understanding of the role of "style." It is equally important for the player to decide the relative importance of each line within the piece. That is, whether the line is a solo, an important countermelody, or a fairly unimportant accompaniment, and so forth. Each of those decisions will have an effect on the degree and type of stress that the player will use.

Consider Figure 70. The first example is a series of measures in which the downbeat is "properly" stressed. But there is absolutely no shape given to the overall group of eight measures. Such an interpretation would not constitute a phrase, although it would certainly be valid as an accompaniment figure. In the second example there are many seeming contradictions to the simple architecture of the measure. However, individual contradictions are cancelled out if we view the overall phrase. If the third beat of a measure is louder than the downbeat, it is because

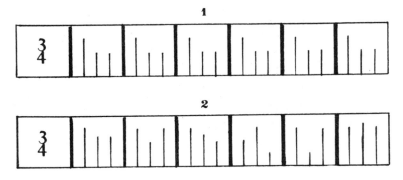

Figure 70. 123

this third beat is leading to a much stronger downbeat in the next measure, and that downbeat had to be prepared. Of course, if the composer had wanted it, the new downbeat could also have been a surprise rather than a culmination. Obviously there are many possibilities open to the composer, and each one of them follows the rules of architectural shaping.

The "flow" of music depends partly upon a certain variety in the phrasing. A single architectural conception for a measure—even when it is a fairly complex one—that is repeated unvaryingly will become mechanical and stand in the way of the flow. The most important factor here is one's understanding and ability to use the various types of stress that exist in music. These, we will remember, consist of time, volume, and vibrato.

The Role of Attack and Release in Stressing Notes

One of the most important factors in the stressing of a note is the type of attack used.

Figure 71 shows the five basic types of attack:
1. The clean attack.
2. The soft attack.
3. The accent.
4. The expressive accent, or *fp*.
5. The sforzando, or *sfz*.

Since the ear is extremely sensitive to minute differences in volume, and since the different types of attack are all examples of different treatments of volume as applied to the beginning of a note, it is clear that the choice of attack has a great deal to do with the amount of stress that the listener perceives. (The composer will usually in-

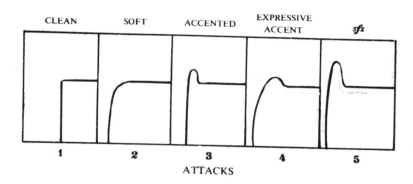

Figure 71.

dictate number (3), (4), or (5), but even when he does, he can only hint at the degree wanted. It must be left to the discretion of the performer). Most of the diagrams are self-explanatory. However, number (4) requires some explanation. This is the forte-piano (*fp*), which we have called an expressive accent. In this type of stress, we want the note in question to be "brought out," but not to be abrupt and surprising, as with the typical accent. The volume increase at the beginning of the note lasts for much longer than it would in the accent. Therefore, the amplitude and duration of the "expressive bulge" would depend on such things in the music as tempo, length of note, the relative importance of the note, and its written dynamic. The regular accent and the *sfz* are much more closely related to each other than is the *fp*, which is meant to be expressive rather than surprising.

The clean attack is inherently one which contains some stress built into it because the note starts at such a very definite point in time. The note appears instantly and at its written dynamic. It is the sudden appearance from nothing that gives the note a degree of stress. The soft attack allows one to start with no stress and is generally used for more "expressive" playing. The soft attack is also possible at a loud dynamic, although it is more difficult to achieve. Used with loud dynamics, it gives the notes a fullness without making them sound "hard." Some people describe such a sound as "sonorous," or "majestic." One of the main points which we will repeatedly state is that the way a person plays must not simply be as a result of his technical deficiencies. He must have many choices open to him and be able to choose the one which is required by the music, rather than be forced to play the only one of which he is capable.

The choice of which release to use is dependent on various musical considerations concerning only the release itself. At the moment we will only consider the release in the context of stressing the next note. Figure 72 shows the five types of release:

1. clean.
2. resonant.
3. short resonant.
4. long resonant.
5. intense.

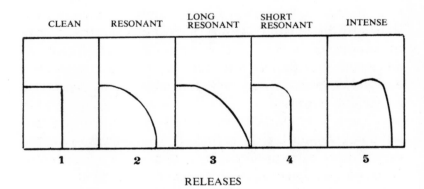

RELEASES

Figure 72.

We know that as far as the attack is concerned, the composer will specify only the various accents. With the release, there is almost a total freedom of choice given to the performer, since there are no signs for the different releases. Even the dot, signifying staccato, does not tell us which ending to use. For our present purposes we can see that the ending of a note can prepare us for the next one, or it can mislead us into expecting something other than what happens. For example, if a note is ended with the long resonant ending, the expectation is for something soft and unaccented, because the long resonance is in effect a dying away of the sound, which is one way of closing off or ending. This may well be our aim, or it might be just the opposite—that is to surprise the listener with the next note. What we have done in that case is to stress the new note by having the last one end "peacefully." In more mechanical terms, this means the new note has started at a louder dynamic than the last one ended and therefore sounds stressed. The longer the resonant ending, the more the new note will sound stressed. Of course it is possible to put any attack and ending together, and indeed it is absolutely essential to have the technique to be able to do so.

The various releases contain within themselves varying degrees of energy. The order from least to most energy is long resonant, resonant, short resonant, clean, and intense. When we apply this concept to the attack, even if the new note is started in exactly the same way, it will sound differently stressed in following each type of release. Find a place in which one phrase ends and a new one immediately begins. Play this example five times, ending the first phrase each time with a different release (long resonant, resonant, short resonant, clean, intense), but always starting the second phrase the same way. The result will be that the amount of stress perceived for the

127

start of the second phrase will be different each time. It would therefore follow, for example, that the way to produce the least amount of stress would be to have the intense ending followed by the soft attack. Some of the possible combinations are quite subtle and take a good deal of practice to achieve. As we said before, the ear is very sensitive to changes in volume, but this is not in an absolute sense. Rather, the sensitivity occurs in comparing one note with another.

Other Ways of Stressing Notes

In addition to being sensitive to small changes in volume, the ear is also as sensitive to small changes in time; not in an absolute sense, however, but rather in comparing one sound with another. In a series of notes, the one which is longest will stand out from the others. This is another prime instance in which the performer is expected to use his "interpretation" in deciding which notes to stress and to what degree. There does not exist a notational device which would indicate that a single note, of the same value as the other notes around it, is to be lengthened. The only sign which even comes close to this is the tenuto mark, −, which usually means to hold the note for its full value, rather than to lengthen it, which results in the note standing out because presumably the other notes were not held for their full values. The idea of lengthening notes is something that is inherent in the musical language, but of course a language has first to be learned so that the player may have an understanding of how much to lengthen them. We must also realize that when a single note is changed, the timing of the rest of the measure is also altered. This can be in one of two ways, the choice being governed by musical considerations. The first involves lengthening the note, and then "catching up" with the other notes so that the beat is not altered and the basic length of the measure remains unchanged. The other is to lengthen the note in the same manner, but not "catch up," which makes the other beats occur later and therefore increases the length of the measure. If the player is part of an ensemble or an orchestra, then it is probably better to use the first method, so that the group will stay together. Of course, if the other players, or the conductor, are sensitive enough, then the choice can be made purely on musical considerations.

Lengthening notes can help to emphasize the architectural structure of a measure. It can also follow the harmonic path of the music, or, in what amounts to the same thing, emphasize those notes that purposely run counter to the harmonic flow. Such a note is often one which clashes with the harmony, as in a suspension.

As we have said before, no one, including the composer, can indicate the exact amount of stress to be used. In the final analysis it is up to the performer's interpretive sensibilities. A performer can destroy the music by pushing it and pulling it out of shape so much that the listener becomes too aware of the distortions, Yet, flexibility is an essential part of the musical language. When the architecture, together with the harmonic flow of a measure, is respected, one is not aware that time is being distorted. Rather one accepts this as the natural flow of the music. It is very much like looking at a picture of a scene; the eye spends more time on those things that are interesting and involving. When the "distorting" is properly done, it is not perceived as a distortion, but as a balance. However, if one were to choose the wrong notes to stress, this would be immediately apparent.

129

Vibrato

Vibrato is the third important way of stressing notes. But in order to be used in this manner it must be completely flexible and under the control of the performer. If this is not so, then the vibrato loses the ability to be more than simply a way to make the tone more pleasant than it would be without vibrato. A tone usually sounds better with vibrato, but it has a purely mechanical function unless it is under the expressive control of the player so that it can change as the needs of the music change. It should be obvious by now that it is the change from one state to another that impresses itself on the ear. Without change, anything can become dull and uninteresting. This is especially true of vibrato. Given any group of notes, it is the one with a different kind of vibrato from the others that will stand out. Here is a list of ways in which vibrato can be altered, even for one note or part of a note:

1. A faster or slower vibrato.
2. Vibrato with greater or lesser amplitude.
3. The vibrato changing during the course of the note.
4. The use of non-vibrato.

In a general way, we can equate various kinds of vibrato with various emotional states in the music. These categories are obviously oversimplifications, but still there is a general truth in them. For one thing, the greater the amplitude of the vibrato, the more we are aware of it. Excited or intense music calls for a faster vibrato, together with greater amplitude. When we play an accompanying figure, the vibrato should be more peaceful; it should be slower and with less amplitude. A single note can become more intense, or more beautiful, by having the vibrato start from nothing, and then increase both in speed and amplitude to the desired level.

To repeat, the exact degree (in this case, the speed and amplitude) of change to be introduced into the vibrato cannot be notated by the composer. It is left to the performer's taste. As usual, familiarity with style, harmony, and balance is necessary in order for the performer to know how to use vibrato as an expressive tool.

Legato Connections Between Notes

We tend to think of legato playing in much simpler terms than we do tongued notes. There are many different types of tongued notes, but with legato, or slurred notes, there is simply the absence of tonguing. Actually, there is almost as much variety in legato playing as there is in tonguing. It is the existence of this variety which allows for any degree of stress that the player may desire. The range of legato connections extends from completely smooth to almost separated.

Let us first review what is meant by legato. In its simplest form it means a connection between notes in which the tongue is not used and in which the breath does not stop. "Smooth" legato is one of the important types of legato,whose main purpose is not to stress notes. It is also one of the most difficult to achieve and one that many players never fully arrive at. We will remember that each note on a wind instrument has its own settings of air and embouchure. In making the "smooth" connection it is necessary to change the settings instantaneously from one note to the next. This is not so difficult when one is playing stepwise, because the changes from one note to another are slight, but when there are skips involved, it becomes much more difficult. When the changes are not done perfectly, we lose smoothness to a greater or lesser degree. Most players overemphasize the settings for the second note in order to be sure that it will come out, but they do this at the expense of smoothness. We are all familiar with this type of playing and have actually come to accept it as a kind of norm for certain legato passages that contain skips. But while it may be what most players do, it is not necessarily correct, and is basically the result of a lack of technique. When we want to stress notes, that is one thing, but when the music calls for absolutely smooth playing, then we must be able to produce it.

To digress for a moment, one of the basic principles for a performer is to play in the way that the music requires, rather than in the way his lack of technique forces him to do. Too many players develop a "style" of playing based on a particular lack of technique, and therefore force all music to conform to their personal weaknesses. Most are unaware of the forces operating and come to believe that their "style" is purely one of conscious choice rather than unconscious compensation. These personal weaknesses may go well with some music, but they will invariably go badly with other music. A musician should always play as a result of strength rather than weakness.

Figure 73 shows a perfectly smooth legato connection. What makes it smooth is that there is no elapsed time between the ending of the first note and the start of the second one. In actual practice, however, there is usually some time taken between the notes during which

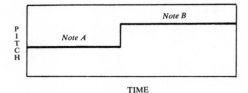

Figure 73.

the new settings are prepared. The more time this takes, the less smooth the connection will be. The technique requires that the changes be as quick as possible and of the proper amount. It is not possible for the changes to be actually instantaneous, but they can be quick enough so that they are not noticed. The bigger the skip, the more difficult, although on each instrument there are certain problem notes that must have special emphasis if they are to come out at all. This particular problem can sometimes be overcome by actually using the tongue in a very discreet way. If this is done properly, it is hard to tell that the tongue has been used. Even when we do hear an extraneous sound, it can often be less disrupting than if the tongue had not been used. The type of tonguing under discussion is what is called long tonguing. As a matter of fact, what is desired here is the longest tonguing possible. The tongue should touch the reed for only the slightest possible instant, so that we don't hear it happen. Even though it is not heard, it has the effect of breaking the air column and making the problem note speak more easily. This is especially true for large downward skips. But remember, this use of the tongue is only for difficult slurred skips, and only as a last resort.

Any deviation from a perfectly smooth connection can be heard and is the basis for the legato emphasizing of notes. Figure 74 shows two examples of "bad" or un-

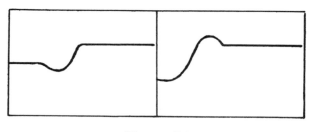

Figure 74.

smooth connections. The bulges represent changes in volume; remember that the ear is especially sensitive to these kinds of changes. Figure 75 shows a passage played with smooth connections and then with connections involving a change in volume. Both are legato, however. The second diagram shows a passage in which each note is emphasized. The emphasis occurs because there is a drop in volume at the end of each note, which causes the next note to give the impression of having begun at a louder dynamic. The drop in volume at the end of the first note cannot go to zero, of course, because there would then be no legato at all.

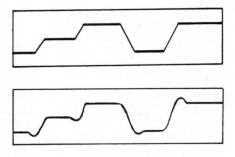

Figure 75.

There are two basic kinds of stressed legato connections: one involves a dropping of the volume for the end of the first note, while the other involves no change at the end of the first note but a greater volume at the beginning of the second. It is also possible to use combinations of these two. Figure 76 gives some examples:

A. This connection slightly stresses the second note.
B. This has the second note brought out more. It is brought out in an "expressive" way. The degree of the "push" can be altered.
C. This is the extreme form of (A), in which the note is so stressed as to almost sound tongued.

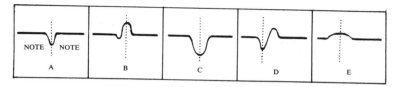

Figure 76.

D. This is similar to the *fp*, or the expressive accent. Notice that *fp* can be written for either a tongued or a slurred note.

E. This will make the connection very strong or obvious.

It is clear that one does not have to tongue a note in order to stress it. As usual, the secret of musical playing is in knowing which notes to stress and in what manner to stress them. Obviously, music does not consist simply in "playing what's on the page." It does consist in the performer interpreting what the composer has put down, and this interpretation must supply all the nuances that the composer had in mind but could not write down because of the inadequacy of notation. The performer can even find things in the music that the composer did not even imagine. This, incidentally, would be one definition of what makes a particular work of art valid: it contains meaning and truth that can be felt and transmitted by people other than the composer. Quite the contrary of "playing what's on the page," the performer has almost unlimited possibilities open to him. We must, however, realize that various musical considerations, in particular style, dictate limitations. Even so, consider the choices in these interpretive areas that are open to the performer:

1. Type of attack.
2. Type of release.
3. Speed, amplitude, and changeability of vibrato.
4. Volume and its changeability.
5. Time and its changeability.

135

6. Articulation, in terms of shortness of notes, and legato connections.

Obviously, any example from each group could be combined with any example from any other group, and these combinations may change from note to note or measure to measure.

All that we have written will not insure that one will play musically. We have taken music apart only to show its various building blocks. These then become the tools which must be used in the making of music. The analogy with language has been used before but it is still very appropriate. The building blocks are like words, and it is up to the performer to combine them much as a writer combines words. There is always a choice, but it is never an indiscriminate one. The choice is vast and is only limited by the imagination and sensibility of the writer or performer.

A Practical Example

Figure 77 shows part of a bassoon solo from the slow movement of Tchaikovsky's Symphony No. 4, as the composer notated it. Then an attempt is made to show the various building blocks. This illustrates only one idea about the musical way in which the phrase might be played. It is by no means the only way.

Whatever way a note is played in a phrase will influence the rest of the phrase. Yet at each note there is a choice of which direction to go. Notes must follow each other in an organic way, even though sometimes we deliberately want to fool the listener. There is never only one path to follow in music, but there must remain a path. Whether it is obvious or misleading, smooth or tortuous, gentle or violent, ugly or beautiful, it must have a begin-

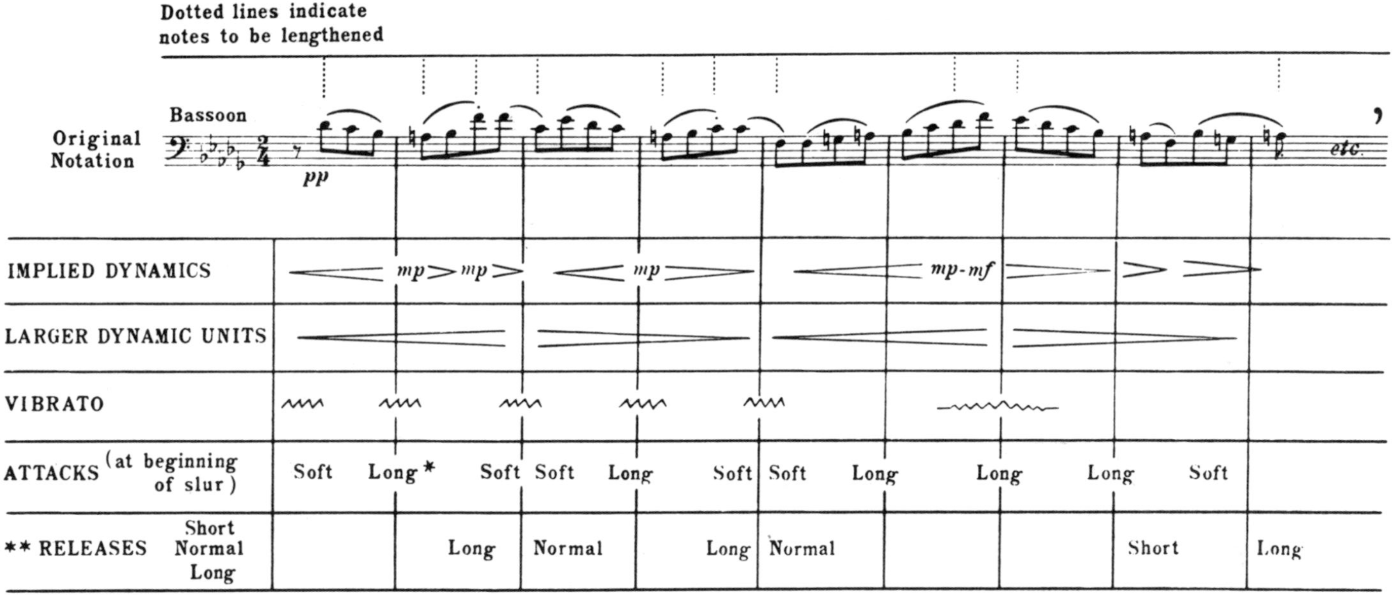

Dotted lines indicate
notes to be lengthened

Original Notation — Bassoon

pp ... *etc.*

IMPLIED DYNAMICS	mp > mp	mp	mp - mf				
LARGER DYNAMIC UNITS							
VIBRATO							
ATTACKS (at beginning of slur)	Soft Long*	Soft Soft Long	Soft Soft Long	Soft Long	Long	Long Soft	
**RELEASES Short / Normal / Long	Long Normal	Normal	Long Normal			Short	Long

* LONG - as little space as possible between notes

** REFERS TO TYPES OF RESONANCE

Figure 77.

137

ning and an end. One does not have to know beforehand where the path will lead, only that it will go somewhere. A beautifully played phrase is its own truth.

INDEX

INDEX

amount of air needed for, 92-94

making time for, 90-92

physiology of, 87-90

See also Air

Cadenza, 105

Cage, John, 112

Chance music, 112

Churches, reverberation in, 101

Clarinet

clarity of starting note on, 27

dynamics of, 5, 6

flutter-tonguing of, 114-15

history of

Classical era, 107

Romantic era, 109

open holes on, 70

vibrato and, 57

Classical style, 106-8

Clean attack, 46, 49, 125-26

Combination tones, 113-14

Connecting notes, 12-14

Concentration, 77-79

Contemporary style, 110-16

Contrabassoon, 109

Counterpoint, 101

Crescendo, 9-10

in Classical era, 107

in intense resonance, 43

soft attack compared to, 49-50

Crescendo-diminuendo, 13

practicing, 15

Cutoff (in breathing), 91-92

Cutout, 43-45

Diaphragm, 21

control of, 14

Diaphragm vibrato, 58, 59

Difficult passages, technique for, 74-79

Diminuendo, 9, 10

cutout of, 44-45

practicing, 15

in Classical era, 107

resonance compared to, 37-39

Double-tonguing, *see* Tonguing—double

Downbeat, 121-24

Drum, resonance of, 33-34

Dynamics, 4-8

fingering and, 83

history of

Baroque era, 105-6

Renaissance lack of flexibility in, 98-100

Romantic era, 109

Embouchure

air and, 3-4, 6-7

fingering, 79-82, 113-14

in Classical era, 107

control of, 14

"no embouchure" playing, 5

quick breathing and, 92

See also specific topics

Embouchure vibrato, 58

English horn, 109

Expressive attack (accent), 51, 125

Families of instruments, 98-99, 102

Fast notes, tonguing, 25

Fingering

choice of, 82-85

"false," 84-85

new, 113-14

slur, 80

Piano
in Classical era, 104
resonance of, 34-35, 36
Piccolo, 109
Pitch
air-embouchure effects on, 8,
30-31
fingering and, 82, 83, 85
influenced by previous note,
13
interpretation and, 119
"perfect," 120

Quivre, 110

Ranges, expansion of, 113
Ravel's *Bolero,* 75
Recorder
fixed mouthpiece of, 4, 99
flute's superiority over, 103-4
Reed instruments
double-tonguing impossible
for, 26
history of
Baroque era, 103-4
Renaissance, 99-100
Romantic era, 109
lack of resonance of, 36
Reeds
dynamics of, 4-8
special, for extreme-range
passages, 33
types of, 3-4
See also Tonguing
Release
exercises in, 55-56
in stressing notes, 124-28
types of, 55
Renaissance style, 98-101
Resonance, 33-43
definition of, 33
intense, 43, 126

short vs. long, 4?
to avoid cutout, 44-45
Reverberation
of churches, 101
resonance compared to, 39
Romantic style, 108-10

Schoenberg, Arnold, 111, 114
Sforzando attack, 50-51, 125
in Romantic era, 109
Short note, *see* Staccato
Singers, vibrato technique of,
58-59
Single-tonguing, *see*
Tonguing—single
Skips, 131-33
use of, 116
Slur fingerings, 80
Slurred notes, *see* Legato playing
Soft attack, 47-50, 125
Soft notes
ending of difficult, 43-45
See also Dynamics
Sonata allegro, 107
Speed, 120-21
Staccato (short note), 18-20,
24-25
history of
Classical era, 107
Romantic era, 110
Strauss, Richard, 114
Stravinsky, Igor, 111
Stress, 122-31, 135
attack and release in, 124-28
by lengthening, 128-29
by vibrato, 130-31
Stringed instruments
attack on, 47-48
history of
Baroque era, 102-3
Classical era, 107
Contemporary era, 114